Summer Lies

THE
SILVER BEACH
TRILOGY

Summer Lies

DIANE SCHWEMM

BANTAM BOOKS
NEW YORK • TORONTO • LONDON • SYDNEY • AUCKLAND

RL 6.0, AGES 012 AND UP

SUMMER LIES

A Bantam Book/June 2005
First Bantam Books Edition August 1995

Copyright © 1995 by Daniel Weiss Associates, Inc., and Diane Schwemm
Cover art copyright © 2005 by Daly & Newton/GETTY
and Mecky/Photonica

ISBN: 0-553-56720-9

Visit us on the Web! www.randomhouse.com/teens
Educators and librarians, for a variety of teaching tools,
visit us at www.randomhouse.com/teachers

Published simultaneously in the United States and Canada

Bantam Books is an imprint of Random House Children's Books, a division
of Random House, Inc. BANTAM BOOKS and the rooster colophon are
registered trademarks of Random House, Inc.

Printed in the United States of America

OPM   10 9 8 7 6 5 4 3 2

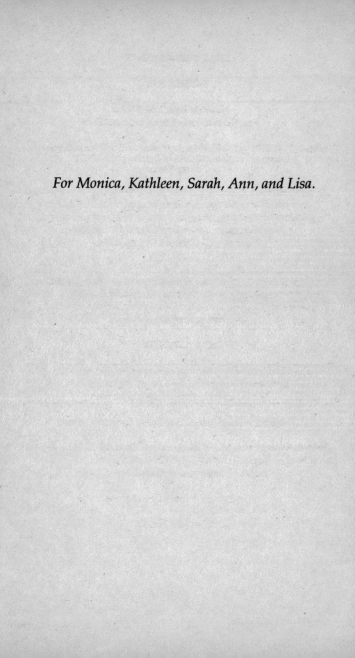

For Monica, Kathleen, Sarah, Ann, and Lisa.

Seventeen-year-old Elli Wells woke with a start. The morning sun slanted through her window, bright and high. *I overslept,* she thought, scrambling out of bed. *My alarm must not have gone off. I'll be late for—*

Then she remembered, and fell back on the bed, stretching and laughing. *It's summer. I can sleep all day if I feel like it.* It was tempting, but as her eyelids drooped closed again she remembered something else. Her junior year in high school was over and vacation had started, but that wasn't all. That day was special for another reason. She was going to Silver Beach.

Silver Beach. Just thinking about it made her feel like a kid. Infused with energy, Elli jumped into the shower, threw on an oversized T-shirt and a pair of khaki shorts, and trotted downstairs to the kitchen. To her surprise, her younger brother was already up, slouched at the table with a big glass of orange juice, a bowl of cereal, and the *Chicago Tribune* sports section. "Cubs won. Extra innings."

Elli dropped into a chair. "That's all the news?"

"Yeah. That and the fact that the weather's great. Especially over on the Michigan side of the lake." Sixteen-year-old Ethan lowered the paper, the corners of his green eyes crinkling slyly. "Wind's up, perfect for sailing."

Elli bounced restlessly in her seat. "So, what are we waiting for? Are you packed?"

"I am, but Mom's not even close to being ready yet. Don't worry." Ethan laughed at his sister. "We'll get there."

Elli smiled. "I can't help it. You'd think after all these years, it wouldn't be such a big deal, going back to Silver Beach, but it is."

He nodded. "I know."

Elli propped her elbows on the table, her chin cupped in her hands. She and Ethan had spent every summer of their lives at their grandparents' sprawling house in Silver Beach, a colony of elegant Victorian cottages on the Lake Michigan shore. It was a timelessly beautiful place, a magical place, and yet not immune, Elli had learned the previous summer, to the forces of change. "This summer will be *really* different," she reflected out loud.

Ethan slurped some orange juice. "Yeah. It'll

be weird not having Dad drive up with us."

Mr. and Mrs. Wells had been separated since the previous autumn. Though they hadn't filed for divorce yet, Elli and Ethan assumed it was just a matter of time. "I wish they'd get it over with," said Elli. "Make their breakup official, I mean. End the suspense."

"Then the fun really starts. Who gets the house, who gets us, all that crap."

"They won't fight about it," Elli predicted, twisting a strand of chin-length brown hair around her finger. "They don't fight about anything anymore, have you noticed? They're so much happier now that they're not living together. The way I see it, we'll go on doing what we're doing right now. Dad has the apartment downtown, so Mom will keep the house and we'll stay in Winnetka with her. We'll see Dad on weekends and he'll put us through college and it won't get weird. It'll all be totally, disgustingly civilized."

"Ain't divorce grand," Ethan agreed sarcastically.

Elli crossed to the counter to grab a piece of toast and pour herself some coffee. She understood Ethan's bitterness; obviously, if given a choice, she'd have preferred her family to stay intact. But there hadn't been a choice. "You have to admit it's better than it used to be around here," she said to her brother. "At least it's peaceful."

"It's just strange thinking Dad won't be at Silver Beach," said Ethan, "not this summer and not ever again."

"But Laura's coming," Elli pointed out. "Doesn't that make up for it?"

At the mention of his girlfriend's name, a smile creased Ethan's face. "Yeah. I guess it does."

For a while they ate breakfast in companionable silence. *What a difference a year makes,* Elli thought, munching her toast. *For both of us.* Junior year had been a good one. She'd gotten straight A's, and her field hockey and lacrosse teams both had had winning seasons. As for her social life, it was definitely an improvement over sophomore year. She'd had a lot of dates—one of the guys, a cute senior named Josh Miller, had even qualified as a real boyfriend for a while. It was a relief to be over the shy-and-inexperienced stage; Elli felt as if she'd hit her stride. But the biggest change was in Ethan's life.

Elli voiced her thought out loud. "I didn't think you'd ever get over Charlotte."

"Neither did I." Ethan frowned, and his sister guessed he was thinking back to the previous fall and how he'd moped and mourned over Charlotte Ransom, the summer love who hadn't returned his phone calls or answered his letters. Then the frown dissolved. "But I didn't think I'd ever meet anyone like Laura, either."

Elli approved wholeheartedly of Ethan's new

girlfriend, Laura McIver. Like Charlotte, Laura was beautiful, but she was also sweet, steady, and down-to-earth. Most important, she genuinely cared for Ethan. No doubt about it, Elli thought: Laura was a miracle. In the two months that the two had been dating, Laura had managed to cure Ethan of his obsession with Charlotte, something Elli hadn't dreamed was possible. "She's the real thing, isn't she?" Elli said softly.

Ethan nodded. "With Charlotte, it was . . . we were . . ." He let the sentence trail off, shrugging as if there weren't words to describe their relationship. "It was beyond intense," he finally said quietly. "I didn't think I was capable of caring about anyone a fraction as much, you know? But with Laura, it's something else altogether. Easier. Better. More . . . real." Ethan laughed, looking a little embarrassed. "Sorry to get so drippy. Might as well let you read my diary, huh?"

Elli smiled as she poured herself some more juice. She didn't pursue the topic; she didn't need to. Ethan truly loved Laura, and that was another reason it was going to be a very different kind of summer at Silver Beach. *As for* my *love life . . .* For a moment Elli let her thoughts dwell on Sam DeWitt. Then she pushed him firmly from her mind. She wouldn't know until she got to Silver Beach what romantic prospects, if any, it might hold for her this summer.

*   *   *

Five hours after leaving Winnetka, Mrs. Wells exited the highway and steered the dark green Range Rover onto a local road. "It's so beautiful around here," Laura McIver observed from the backseat. "We're really in the country."

Elli looked out the window, imagining it was she who was seeing the landscape for the first time. On either side of the road, meadows and orchards were bright with blossoms and new grass; in the distance, wooded hills undulated like waves. The air coming in the window smelled as crisp and fresh as an apple.

"Here's Silver Glen," Ethan told Laura. "The town where we buy groceries and stuff."

"Bee's Bakery, Harlan's Boat Repair, Christabel's House of Beauty." Laura read the signs out loud, laughing. "Kind of different from the strip malls back home in the 'burbs."

"But they've got everything you need," Ethan swore. "Bailey's Bait and Tackle—best crawlers in the county."

"Ugh," said Laura. "I knew there was a reason I was never into fishing."

"Don't worry, there are plenty of other things to do," Mrs. Wells told her. "Tennis, golf, swimming, boating. Silver Beach is a country club, basically, but with a million times more character."

After passing through the village, they drove through farmland for a few more miles. Then the

Range Rover crested a windswept hill. Elli caught her breath, as she always did, at her first sight of the sparkling, sapphire-blue lake, as wide and endless as an ocean. "There it is!" she cried.

They swooped back down the hill and Mrs. Wells tapped the brakes. The sign marking the entrance to Silver Beach looked more weather-beaten than ever. "And you'd think they could pave this road," Mrs. Wells grumbled cheerfully as the car rattled along the gravel. "One of these centuries!"

The summer colony unfolded before them. Tennis courts and golf course, the yacht club at one end of an expansive emerald lawn overlooking the docks and the cove, and finally the cottages themselves. Some were fanciful gingerbread houses, authentic Victorian "painted ladies" adorned with porches and turrets and gables; others were more staid and dignified, content simply to be gracious and large. All had one thing in common: they'd stood facing the lake, shutters open to the summer sun and flags snapping proudly in the breeze, for more than a hundred years.

"They're enormous," Laura gasped.

"Three stories, most of them," agreed Mrs. Wells. "People had big families back then—eight, ten children, plus servants."

She turned the Range Rover into the driveway of a sprawling, gray-shingled mansion. "And here we are. Home."

Home. *It is home to her, more than Winnetka ever could be,* Elli reflected. *Before Ethan and I were born, before she met Dad, Mom had Silver Beach. She grew up here.*

At the sound of the approaching car, a silver-haired woman wearing overalls and a floppy straw hat looked up from her gardening. She waved, then walked toward them, removing her earth-smudged gloves as she came. Elli was the first to embrace her. "Nana!"

Eleanor Chapman returned her granddaughter's hug. "Elli," she said, her voice brimming with emotion. "Oh, isn't it going to be good to have you all here with me."

"Mother, you look wonderful," Grace Wells said approvingly. "The picture of health."

"Yeah, have you been lifting weights, Nana?" Ethan kidded.

"It's that triathlon I'm training for," Mrs. Chapman joked back. Then her piercing green eyes settled on Laura. "You must be Ethan's friend. I'm so glad to meet you."

"It's nice of you to invite me," Laura replied with a smile.

Mrs. Chapman gestured at the house. "As you can see, there are plenty of spare rooms. Filling them up makes me happy. So, come along inside. You too, Rasta," she said, addressing the Wellses's black Labrador retriever.

They each grabbed a couple of suitcases and

walked along the flagstone path to the house. As she drew near, a lump formed in Elli's throat. The house looked the same as always, rambling and tall with a wraparound porch and windows open everywhere. In fact, with a new coat of dove-gray paint, it looked better than ever, cheerful and almost new. But no coat of paint could change the fact that one of the pine rockers on the porch would always be empty, rocked only by the lake breeze.

Elli swallowed her tears. She didn't want to get emotional—that wasn't what her grandmother needed from her. But it was impossible not to remember how the previous summer had ended, with her ailing grandfather's sudden death. Elli missed Grandpa Chapman all the time, but the pang was infinitely sharper here, as she stepped into the house of which he had been so much a part.

She, Ethan, and Laura clomped to the staircase with their bags. As she started up Elli glanced over her shoulder. Her mother and grandmother stood in the doorway to the library that had been Horace Chapman's favorite room. Mrs. Wells had her arms around Mrs. Chapman. There were tears on both their faces. Elli turned away from the sight, her own eyes stinging.

Ethan's room was the first off the upstairs hallway. "This is the one Nana fixed up for you," he said to Laura, escorting her to the

9

guest bedroom down the hall, next to Elli's room. "You get a lake view."

Elli followed them, peeking into Laura's room. Laura dropped her suitcases on the bed and ran to the window to look out. "It's magnificent," she said breathlessly. "I can't believe this place is real. Do you guys know how lucky you are?"

Elli exchanged a glance with Ethan. "Yeah, I think we do," she said.

Five minutes later, Elli was unpacking in her own room when Laura tapped on the door. "Come on in," Elli invited.

"This is a cute room," Laura remarked, sitting down on the overstuffed easy chair and resting her feet on the matching ottoman.

"I love it," Elli admitted. She looked around at the twin beds made up with crisp white spreads, the curtained dormers opening out to the front lawn and the lake, the richly burnished cherry furniture. "See that trunk against the wall? It's full of antique dolls. A long time ago, I put a couple of my tacky old Barbies in there for good measure."

Laura laughed. "It's funny to think of you and Ethan here as little kids."

"My family's been here forever," said Elli. "I mean, my mom's family, the Chapmans. It's been their summer place since the beginning of time, practically—that's the kind of place it is."

Laura sat forward, hugging her knees. "Tell

10

me about it," she urged. "Tell me about the people I'm going to meet."

Elli paused in her unpacking. "First of all, everyone's . . . how shall I put it?"

"Filthy rich?" suggested Laura with a smile.

Elli laughed. "Old families, old money. Fortunately, we only have it from one side—my dad's background isn't quite so preppy. I'd hate to be a total snob."

"The white house to the north," Laura prompted.

"Gull Cottage," said Elli. "Old Mr. and Mrs. Emerson live there. They're very sweet—they have three cats and they play croquet. Their son Bob bought a cottage farther down the point—he has a couple of kids. Chad's my age and Julia's in college."

"Are there a lot of high-school and college kids?"

"Tons," said Elli, ticking them off on her fingers. "Becky, Bradley, and Jack Nichols, Tim and Heather Courtland, Hugh and Libby Lowell, Sam DeWitt"—she wondered if Laura noticed that her cheeks turned pink when she mentioned Sam's name—"Doug Fairleigh, the Branfords have three, and of course the Madden twins, Amber and Amelia." Elli rolled her eyes expressively. "The colony gossips. Between the two of them, they don't miss a trick. They'll be checking you out at the party tonight, so be prepared."

Laura laughed. "I can handle it. But you

know, of course, the one I'm *really* dying to meet is the infamous Charlotte Ransom."

"The infamous Charlotte Ransom." Elli laughed, somewhat uneasily. "Well, there's no way to avoid her, that's for sure. She lives right next door."

Laura smiled. "Don't worry, Elli. I really don't feel threatened."

"You shouldn't," said Elli, relaxing. "Ethan's over Charlotte, and he's crazy about you."

Yes, Laura had nothing to be afraid of. *And neither do I—none of us do,* Elli decided. Charlotte had always been cruel and manipulative; she'd broken plenty of hearts, including Ethan's, and she'd probably break many more. But Ethan was out of danger now. He was a stronger person, thanks in large part to Laura. Charlotte's reign was over.

"A little overwhelming, isn't it?" Ethan asked Laura as he steered her toward the bar.

"I just know I'm going to forget everyone's name," said Laura. "And how will I ever tell Amelia and Amber apart?"

Ethan laughed. "Don't worry about it. There's plenty of time to get it straight—you'll be hanging out with these people all summer."

"That Sam guy's really cute. I got the feeling he was looking around for your sister. What's the story there?"

"Good question. You'll have to ask Elli."

The cocktail party at the Silver Beach Yacht Club was in full swing, with adults socializing in the building's larger room, known as the Big Club, and younger colony residents filling the smaller Little Club. Ethan bought sodas at the bar, then grabbed Laura's hand. "Come on. Let's go out on the deck and watch the sunset."

They went to the edge of the deck and leaned against the railing. "Don't get me wrong," Laura said to Ethan. "I really liked everybody I met. I feel at home already."

"I knew you'd fit right in," he replied.

He *had* known. Laura was so easygoing—she got along with everybody. *At home,* thought Ethan, gazing at her profile. That's the way he'd felt around her right from the start. He'd met her through Elli—the two girls were on the same lacrosse team—and at first they'd been just buddies who liked hanging out together. Gradually their relationship had become more serious. *That's what I like about Laura,* Ethan concluded. *There's no pressure.* She'd never made him trip over his feet or stumble over his words. He wanted her to love Silver Beach, but he didn't feel he had to do stunts to impress her.

Below them, the cove had sunk into dusky gray; Blueberry Island, at the mouth of the channel, was dim and shadowed. Across the dunes in the distance, Lake Michigan was edged with silver

13

where it met the sky, which flamed above it in brilliant shades of orange, red, and purple. "You couldn't get away with painting a sky that dramatic and beautiful," murmured Laura, close to his side. "People would say it looked fake."

Ethan turned toward her. The last rays of the sinking sun warmed her skin and brought out the gold lights in her brown eyes. "Speaking of beautiful—"

The words died in his throat. Across the deck, Ethan saw her. The girl stood silhouetted against the sky, every sensuous curve of her body outlined, her wavy honey-blond hair billowing in the breeze. He caught his breath. Charlotte.

For a split second, Ethan was certain his heart stopped beating. Charlotte was, if anything, more spectacularly gorgeous than ever. Her hair was longer, blonder, her figure riper and more womanly. He could see the luster of her tanned skin and imagine its softness, its seductive fragrance. The deep blue pools of her eyes, the full curve of her lips—he knew every feature, every inch of her beautiful body.

His hand tightened on the rough wood of the railing. Scenes of their togetherness flashed before his eyes as if he were drowning. The first unforgettable kiss the previous summer during the Fourth of July fireworks. Making love in the sun on a bed of pine needles on Blueberry Island.

Meeting every single night after dark—his house, her house, the dock, the beach, wherever they could be alone—then talking and kissing and touching for hours and hours.

Slowly Ethan's eyes refocused. Charlotte continued to stand, unmoving, but the reawakened feelings faded. Yes, he had powerful memories of his love for Charlotte, but he had equally powerful memories of the pain she'd caused him, the betrayal. *Memories,* Ethan thought. *That's all they are—that's all she is.*

Laura had seen Charlotte, too; she was waiting patiently. Ethan took her hand and gave it a firm squeeze. Warmth and encouragement flowed into his body from hers, and the contrast grew ever clearer. Where Charlotte had reduced him to rubble, Laura gave him strength, self-confidence. "There's someone I'd like you to meet," Ethan said.

My God, she's beautiful, Laura thought. As Ethan led her in Charlotte's direction Laura's heart started to flutter with trepidation. Suddenly, despite what she'd said to Elli that afternoon, she was nervous about meeting Ethan's ex-girlfriend. She'd pictured Charlotte as pretty, but never in a million years had she summoned up a vision like this.

Charlotte's short, clingy knit dress made it easy to appreciate her every curve. She was built like a fashion model—tall with long legs, a slim waist, and full breasts. Laura had a decent figure herself, but she couldn't help feeling scrawny in comparison. And the honey-blond hair falling in glamorous waves down Charlotte's back, the wide-set blue eyes, the full, red lips—not even the word *beautiful* really did her justice.

"Charlotte, uh, hi," said Ethan, his voice cracking slightly as he and Laura came to a stop. "It's nice to see you. You really look—" He turned to Laura, as if for help. "Um, this is my . . . friend, Laura. Laura McIver."

"Hi, Charlotte. Nice to meet you," said Laura, holding out her hand.

Charlotte gave it a perfunctory shake. "Laura McIver," she mused, her voice low and velvety. "I don't think I've heard that name before."

The brilliant blue eyes were on Ethan, probing and intense. Again, he turned away from them, facing Laura. "It's been a while since we were in touch, Char," he pointed out, "and Laura and I only met—what, a couple of months ago?"

"April," Laura confirmed.

Charlotte's gaze shifted to Laura, taking in her appearance from head to toe. The scrutiny made Laura feel awkward and plain—her dress was wrong, her hair, her jewelry, her shoes. "And you're here for the Fourth of July weekend, Laura?"

"Actually, Ethan invited me to spend the whole summer," Laura replied.

16

For an instant a look of displeased surprise flashed across Charlotte's face. Then her lips curled in a cool, half-mocking smile. "The whole summer. Isn't that nice. Then we'll probably be bumping into each other all the time—we're neighbors, you know."

Laura smiled back, though she was starting to wish that Charlotte Ransom's cottage was located at the other end of the colony. "Yes, I know."

"Well . . ." Ethan shifted his weight from one foot to the other. "There are a bunch more people Laura needs to meet. See you around, Char."

"See you," Charlotte echoed, turning on her heel and stalking away.

Laura watched Charlotte go. Next to her, Ethan's whole body was as taut as a bowstring. "I'm glad we got that over with," he admitted.

Laura bit her lip. "Me too."

"It wasn't so bad, was it?"

"No." As she looked into Ethan's eyes, though, she couldn't help feeling a momentary twinge of insecurity. Meeting Charlotte was like looking through a window into another world, another life Ethan had lived before Laura came along. His past. *And it's different from my past, my old boyfriends,* Laura realized, *because it's here. She's here.* As Charlotte had seemed only too happy to point out, she lived right next door.

Ethan had fully recovered his composure. Laura brushed away the flicker of concern, but not before a tiny doubt had been implanted in her brain. *I didn't think I had anything to worry about. Maybe I was wrong.*

Elli smoothed her hands nervously down her slim-fitting navy-and-white flowered dress. *I should've worn something shorter, sexier,* she thought, wishing there were time to duck into the ladies' room and see if her hair was totally limp and lifeless. *And jewelry and makeup.* A second later she seesawed to the opposite conviction. *No, I should've just worn jeans. These heels are ridiculous—I can't walk, and I look like a giant.*

But it was clearly too late to fuss over her appearance. From across the room, Sam DeWitt caught her eye and waved. As he made his way toward her, pushing past the crowds, Elli felt her heart pound. He was nineteen, two years older than Elli. Tall and well-built, with broad shoulders and lean hips, he wore khaki trousers, a navy blazer, a white oxford shirt, and a tie, but Elli couldn't help picturing him in swim trunks. Already he had a good tan, and his chestnut hair was sun-bleached. As he approached her he smiled warmly, the corners of his hazel eyes crinkling. "Elli! How've you been?"

She didn't know whether to shake his hand or give him a peck on the cheek. He solved the dilemma for her by folding her in a friendly bear hug that left her breathless. "Fine," she gasped. "How 'bout you?"

"Good, good. So tell me—"

"We need you, DeWitt," Forrest Madden interrupted as he strode over. "Hi, Elli. Mind if I borrow him?"

"He's all yours," Elli replied.

Sam smiled apologetically. "I'll catch up with you later, okay?"

"Sure." For an instant he held her eye, and Elli felt a flash of heat course through her body. Then he was gone.

She'd thought a lot about Sam over the winter, but they hadn't communicated except for Christmas cards. She'd had the urge to call him a couple of times, but she'd never known what to say, where they stood with each other. Now, as she watched Sam disappear into the crowd, Elli remembered their kiss the previous summer, the night of the Midsummer Madness costume ball, and her cheeks flushed. It had been her first kiss ever, and still rated as the most earth-shaking by far—even Josh Miller didn't come close. But instead of being the start of something, Midsummer Madness had brought their romance to a dead halt. Elli had been distraught over her parents' disintegrating marriage, her grandfather's failing health, and the discovery that Charlotte was cheating on Ethan. She'd run away from Sam, unable to deal with the new, adult emotions the kiss had summoned up.

But there was no doubt about it now. She was wild about Sam, always had been. She had blown it the summer before, but maybe now she was mature enough to handle a relationship with him. The big question was: A year after their kiss, was Sam still interested?

How dare he, Charlotte fumed, still enraged an hour after Ethan had introduced Laura to her. How dare Ethan have a new love, and how dare he bring her to Silver Beach and flaunt her in Charlotte's face!

Her eyes sought out Ethan in the crowd just as Forrest Madden, a handsome college junior, stepped to her side. "I'm having a little party later, Char," Forrest said. "Stop by, okay?"

With an effort, Charlotte focused on Forrest. She gave him the teasing half-smile that she knew from long experience drove guys crazy. "Sure. Can I bring anything?"

"Just yourself. And how about we start right now? I'll buy you a drink."

"I'm underage," she reminded him.

Forrest laughed. "Well, I'm not. Stay right here."

He strode off and she watched him go, checking out the view. Forrest wasn't half bad— they'd gone out a couple of times two summers earlier and it had been relatively fun. *He was sniffing around again last summer,* Charlotte recalled, *but then Ethan showed up.* Ethan hadn't been the scrawny asthmatic kid she used to tease and torment, but a young man, all grown up and gorgeous. They'd plunged into a steamy relationship and he'd actually held her interest all summer—well, *almost* all summer. She'd cheated a bit, but she'd still had him firmly wrapped around her finger when he went home at the end of August. What had happened?

Again Charlotte's gaze was drawn like a magnet to Ethan, who was on the other side of the Little Club introducing Laura to more people. A hot tingle stirred deep inside her. Was it possible Ethan was even better-looking than she remembered him?

"Hey, Char, how's it going?"

Charlotte tore her eyes from Ethan as Tim Courtland placed a hand on her arm. He and Doug Fairleigh had just arrived at her side and immediately began talking about summer plans.

"I've been thinking," said Tim. "Why don't we teach tennis together at the day camp?"

"Water-skiing would be a lot more mellow," Doug argued. "And I'm more fun than Courtland any day."

"Come on," Charlotte said playfully. "One of you make me an offer I can't refuse."

But even as she flirted with Tim and Doug her gaze drifted to Ethan. She was startled by the intensity with which she found herself remembering their romance. And what about him? she wondered. What about his memories of the previous summer? What about all the letters he'd written to her at boarding school during the fall? Dozens of them, dripping with anguished longing. And the desperate messages on her answering machine. She hadn't bothered calling or writing back—she hadn't thought she needed to. Hadn't he remained devoted over the years, no matter how poorly she treated him? Hadn't it always been his role to go to desperate measures for her, ever since childhood?

Forrest returned with her drink and Charlotte took it without a word, her brain chasing itself in circles. *He met someone else. He met someone else and he brought her here.* It was unthinkable, but it had happened. Her throat suddenly dry, Charlotte gulped her drink. Deep inside, underneath the heat of her anger and jealousy, something cold squeezed her heart like a fist. Loneliness? Sorrow? Regret? Those were feelings she refused to acknowledge, words she wouldn't let enter her consciousness. But maybe more than her pride was injured. Watching him with Laura McIver, Charlotte perversely found herself wanting Ethan more than ever. Did that mean she actually *loved* him?

2

The next morning dawned fresh and clear and cool, lush with the smell of pines and newly cut grass. Elli couldn't wait to get outside.

Her mother and grandmother were already up, enjoying their coffee in the sunny breakfast room. "I'm going to take my breakfast out to the beach," Elli announced, wrapping a couple of bran muffins in a paper napkin and filling a thermos with coffee. "See you in a bit." She whistled for Rasta as she went out the door. Vaulting past her, he galloped across the lawn to the dunes, scattering gulls.

The damp sand was deliciously cold on Elli's bare feet. She spread out her sweatshirt and sat down facing the lake, then poured some steaming-hot coffee into the thermos cup. Before she could take her first sip, someone called her name. "Elli. Should've known I'd find you out here."

23

Sam was walking down the beach from the north, toes digging deep in the sand with every long stride. Elli waved cheerfully. "Join me for breakfast," she called back.

He dropped down beside her and she offered him a muffin, then the coffee. "I love it here so much," she said, gesturing at the sparkling blue lake. "I could live on the dunes. Who needs a house?"

Sam laughed. "Especially these houses. It's ridiculous, me and my grandfather rattling around all by ourselves in Eagle Cottage. It has, what, seven, eight bedrooms? Five bathrooms? I keep telling him we should rent the place out, move into the carriage house. 'Over my dead body,' he says. Means it, too."

Sam's grandfather, Theodore DeWitt, had made his fortune in the automobile industry. Though Mr. DeWitt owned the largest house in Silver Beach, Sam, whose parents had long ago divorced and married other people, was the only relative who joined him for the whole summer anymore. "How's he doing?" asked Elli.

"Pretty good. I'm sure you'll be seeing a lot of him—he and your grandmother play cards together and stuff. By the way, she looks great."

"She's tough as nails," said Elli. "I think she had a hard winter, but she doesn't dwell on that sort of thing. She focuses on what she still has— the house, the garden, us—not what she lost."

"Good philosophy," remarked Sam.

"And birdwatching. Now that everyone knows about the bald eagles nesting on Blueberry Island . . ."

"Our secret's out, huh?"

"Yeah," Elli said regretfully. "Discovering the nest—why did we keep it a secret, anyway?"

Sam shrugged. "It was more fun. It sort of belonged to us that way."

Elli felt a rush of warmth. *It belonged to us—it was our secret.*

Sam passed the thermos cup to her so she could refill it. Elli took a sip, then handed it back to him. His fingers brushed hers; a shiver chased up her spine. Suddenly Elli realized that she couldn't continue to sit there and pretend that Sam DeWitt was just another guy and her feelings for him were totally platonic. *It's the start of a new summer,* she thought, her pulse racing. *Maybe we'll have a second chance.*

How to bring the conversation around to something more personal, though? She couldn't exactly say, "So, are you going to ask me out or what? Do you still think I'm too young for you?" She seized on a topic that was in the right ballpark, but still relatively safe: someone else's love life. "So what do you think about Laura McIver?" she asked Sam.

"She's adorable," he replied. "Really sweet. Good sense of humor, fantastic smile." He eyed her knowingly. "And she's not Charlotte. That's a big plus, right?"

Elli blushed slightly. "I guess I was a little overprotective of Ethan last summer."

Sam smiled. "A little. Their relationship really bummed you out."

Elli's blush deepened. "It's just that Charlotte has always been so mean to him, ever since they were little kids. Remember the time she hit him over the head with the hammer because he was playing with a toy she wanted?" Elli and Sam had talked about this incident the summer before; for some reason, it was a memory she kept coming back to, a memory that for Elli seemed to sum up Charlotte. "And she obviously hasn't changed one tiny bit over the years. She still doesn't think about other people's feelings, or about what the consequences of her actions are going to be."

"Well, the good news is, Ethan's kicked the habit," Sam pointed out. "If he's not hung up on Charlotte, she can't have any power over him, right?"

"Right," said Elli.

"So, how about you?" Sam nudged her arm with his elbow. "How's the dating scene back in Winnetka?"

Something about the way he asked the question made Elli feel about twelve years old. His tone was teasing, big-brotherly, as if "dating" was just so high-school. *Because he's halfway through college, where people sleep together and have "relationships,"* thought Elli. "It was all right," she said, trying to sound casual, adult. "I kept pretty busy."

"Juggling the boyfriends, huh?"

She laughed. "I don't know about juggling, but there were a few. I mean, why sit home on a Saturday night?"

"Anyone in particular?"

Elli thought about Josh. They'd been nowhere near as serious a couple as Ethan and Laura. On the other hand, it was the closest she'd come to being in love. "Yeah. Josh—Josh Miller. He was a senior, just graduated. I thought about inviting him up here, but . . ." She waved a hand. "You know how it is."

"No, actually, how is it?" Sam smiled, but his eyes were serious.

"Um, how is it?" Elli repeated awkwardly.

"Why didn't you invite him?" Sam pressed. "I mean, you're going out with him, right?"

Elli felt cornered. Why had she even mentioned Josh? She couldn't back away from the story now without looking like an idiot. "Oh, yeah, we are. But—" Her cheeks flamed. "At some point, I might— He might—"

Sam took in her blush, then abruptly put his hands on his knees and stood up. "Listen, I told my grandfather I'd buzz into town and pick up some groceries," he said, his tone suddenly clipped. "See you over at the clubhouse later."

"Yep," said Elli.

"Thanks for breakfast."

"No problem. So long."

Sam jogged off up the beach. Frustrated, Elli tossed the rest of her bran muffin to a seagull. *What was I saying?* she asked herself. She hadn't meant to make it sound as though she and Josh were *married*—she'd only mentioned him at all so Sam would know she wasn't a naive, inexperienced kid anymore. She wanted him to know she was desirable . . . and available. Instead, he'd gotten the opposite impression. "Mixed signals," Elli muttered to the squawking, appreciative gull. "I goofed again."

The clubhouse was crowded with high-school and college-age kids interested in signing up as counselors for the colony day camp. Elli spotted Sam, wearing a Silver Beach Day Camp T-shirt and holding a clipboard, and guessed that he'd taken over the job of giving out assignments.

"What activity do you want to do?" Laura asked Elli.

"Well, last summer Sam and I taught sailing together. We haven't talked about it, but I assume this year we'll—"

She broke off as Sam whistled loudly from

the front of the clubhouse. The chattering stopped. "Let's get this out of the way so we can go outside and meet the campers," he began. "First, Ethan Wells has an announcement."

Ethan gave a salute to acknowledge the attention that had turned his way. "Just wanted to tell everybody that Laura and I will be running an expanded arts program with creative writing and acting." He pointed at Laura and smiled. "Did everybody meet Laura? This was her idea, actually—she does drama club at school. Anyway, the kids'll write and perform their own plays, which should be a lot of fun. I'll post a sign-up sheet for anyone who wants to help us."

Elli couldn't resist checking Charlotte for a reaction. Just as she'd expected, Charlotte looked distinctly pissed. She stood with her weight on one leg and a hand on her hip, narrowed eyes glaring at Laura. *If looks could kill,* Elli thought, amused.

A few moments later, Sam was soliciting volunteers for various camp activities. "So, first we have soccer and tennis." People raised their hands, and Sam jotted down their names. "How about canoeing and water safety?" More hands went up. "Okay, what's left? Sailing. Elli, you're the best-qualified. Interested?"

"You bet," she responded promptly.

"Good." He made a note. "I need one more person for sailing. Who feels up to the job?"

"What about you?" Elli blurted out. "Last

29

year—" She caught herself, hoping she hadn't given too much away.

"I feel like I've been hogging all the glory," Sam explained. "It's someone else's turn, you know? I'm doing water-skiing instead, with Julia."

Elli swallowed her surprise and disappointment. So Sam was teaching water-skiing with one of his old girlfriends, Julia Emerson, who with her sleek auburn hair, slate-gray eyes, and classic features was the most elegant girl in Silver Beach. Elli shot a glance at Julia just in time to intercept a look between her and Sam. Something about the way they smiled at each other made Elli's heart drop into her sneakers. This was nothing like day camp sign-up day the previous summer, when Sam had specifically requested Elli as his co-instructor, when he had asked her to sail with him in the annual Midsummer Madness regatta.

"So, any volunteers to help Elli with sailing?" Sam asked, scanning the crowd. His eyes settled on Charlotte. "Char, you need something to do, right? And you're pretty handy with boats."

Charlotte glanced at Elli with ill-concealed distaste. "No, thanks."

Sam tapped his pen on the clipboard. "It's either sailing or this new writing-and-drama workshop," he informed Charlotte. "Take your pick."

"I guess I'll do sailing, then," Charlotte muttered.

Elli stifled a groan. Like it or not, she and Charlotte were stuck together. *Looks like it's going to be a great summer,* she thought with a sigh.

"It's all so beautiful," Laura said to Ethan that afternoon. "I can see why you love it."

After camp wrapped up for the day, Ethan had decided to take Laura on a grand tour of Silver Beach. They'd walked past the tennis courts and over the golf course, through the meadows, and back to the gravel road that ran down the length of the peninsula to Eagle Cottage, the imposing DeWitt mansion. Now they were canoeing across the still waters of the cove toward Blueberry Island.

"It's special," Ethan agreed. "I know every tree, every rock, every patch of beach like the back of my own hand. You could drop me anywhere in the colony, blindfolded, and I'd be able to tell exactly where I was and find my way home."

"I can't imagine feeling that way about a place," Laura confessed as she dipped her paddle into the water. "We moved around so much when I was a kid—sometimes we took a summer vacation, sometimes we didn't. I feel like we've lived in Winnetka forever, and it's been only three years."

"Well, you'll get to know Silver Beach this summer," Ethan promised, "and if you like it, maybe next summer . . ."

31

She turned, her glossy hair swinging, and smiled at him over her shoulder. "Thanks," she said softly. "For bringing me here. For sharing this."

Ethan bent forward carefully, so as not to rock the canoe, and touched her arm. "I'm the one who should be thanking you."

They landed the canoe on the small island's south beach, then walked into the trees. "There's a bald eagles' nest on the other side," Ethan told Laura. "Elli and Sam found it last summer."

The eagles were nesting in the same dead pine, and Ethan and Laura got a good look at both of the majestic adult birds. "If we come back in a week or two, the babies will have hatched," he said. "That'll be a sight."

Hand in hand, they made their way back to the beach. Ethan sat on the sand, pulling Laura down next to him. "This is why I really brought you here," he teased, nuzzling her neck. "It's a great place to make out."

Laura pushed him away, laughing. "Yeah, in full view of anyone in the cove."

"I don't see any boats," he said, wrapping both arms around her waist. "So why don't we—"

He felt Laura's body tense. She was staring straight out at the water; he sat up to follow her gaze. A lone Sunfish skated across the surface of the cove, its sail round with wind. There was a girl in a skimpy red bikini at the tiller, her long blond hair streaming out behind her.

Ethan couldn't tell if Charlotte had spotted them. He and Laura watched the boat until it disappeared into the channel on the other side of the island, heading for the open lake. "She makes you uncomfortable," Ethan said after a moment, breaking the silence.

Laura shook her head. "Not really. But I can't help wondering if, seeing her again, you feel any . . . I mean, you used to come here with *her,* didn't you?"

Ethan couldn't deny it. "We grew up here together, me and Charlotte," he said. "But I bet you and I can figure out how to get away from those old memories." He pulled Laura close, gazing earnestly into her eyes. "When I'm with you, you're all I think about. And when I'm *not* with you, you're all I think about. You're the only one, Laura."

She smiled, her eyes warm. "Prove it," she whispered.

Ethan's hands tightened on her back and he lowered his mouth to hers, kissing her gently at first and then with more passion and urgency—more than he'd ever felt with Laura before. Lost in the heat of the embrace, they did become, for a moment, the only two people in Silver Beach, the only two people in the world.

Charlotte trudged across the grass toward Briarwood, a baggy T-shirt clinging to her damp body and her sandals in her hand. The solitary sail and swim had tired her out physically, but they'd done nothing to dull the sharp edges of her angry, frustrated mood.

Briarwood had been in her father's family for generations. For almost a decade, since the drowning death of her mother and her novelist father's decision to live year-round in Silver Beach, it had been Charlotte's only home. It was a graceful, lovely house embellished with porches and balconies, floor-to-ceiling windows, and airy turrets, but she wasn't sure if she loved or hated it. During those long, cold, lonely winters it had seemed like a prison, from which boarding school had finally freed her. Not that Bedford Hall was the promised land. *Now I just go back and forth from one prison to another,* thought Charlotte, disgruntled, as she dropped her sandals on the porch and stomped inside, letting the screen door bang behind her.

Holling Ransom was in the kitchen, on the telephone. "I'll be ready to let you look at this draft in, oh, let's say a month."

His editor, Charlotte guessed, opening the fridge and reaching in for a bottle of fruit-flavored seltzer.

"I know, I know," Mr. Ransom continued. "We want to publish late next spring and do the book tour in the summer, but you know how I work. The story runs me, not the other way around."

She sat down at the table and used the hem of her T-shirt to twist off the bottle cap. A few minutes later, her father said good-bye and replaced the receiver. "She's putting the screws on you, huh?" Charlotte observed brightly.

Her tall, lean father raked a hand through his silver-streaked black hair. "She's good at what she does—the best. But there's a reason she's editing fiction, not writing it."

"She doesn't understand the creative process," Charlotte commiserated. "It must really bug you when . . ." She didn't bother finishing the sentence. Her father had left the room; his footsteps echoed down the hallway and then his study door slammed.

That hateful novel. Charlotte tipped the bottle back, draining its fizzy contents. Tears stung her eyes and she wiped them away angrily. What was the point of feeling slighted and abandoned? Her father cared more about his writing than he ever had about any person, living or dead—that wasn't exactly news.

Rising to her feet, she tossed the empty bottle in the recycling bin and paced restlessly out to the deck. The sun balanced on the horizon in a pool of blazing orange, poised to sink into the lake. Charlotte gazed to the north, at the Chapman cottage. The shade in Ethan's window was down—the shade he used to raise and lower as a signal that he wanted to see her. Needed to see her. Couldn't wait another second to be with her, to hold her, kiss her, make love to her.

Charlotte whirled away from the darkened window next door and from the cold, quiet house she herself lived in and stalked off into the dusk.

"Looking for me?" a voice called out from behind Sam as he walked south along the lake at sunset.

He turned. Charlotte was crossing the dunes, her hair glinting like gold in the last rays of light. He realized his stroll had taken him past the Chapman cottage to the beach in front of Briarwood. He *had* been hoping he might bump into someone, but it wasn't Charlotte. Still, he gave her a friendly smile. "What's up, Char?"

She fell into step beside him. "Not a whole lot," she replied, a note of boredom in her voice. "It's just the start of the season, allegedly the most exciting time, and this place feels totally dead. I should have spent the whole summer in Europe."

Sam refrained from asking if this pronouncement had anything to do with Ethan's desertion. "How's your dad these days?" he asked. "Haven't seen him around."

"Do you ever see him around?" Charlotte rejoined. She jerked her chin, flipping her hair back—a gesture brimming with barely suppressed dissatisfaction. "It's the usual scene. He's holed up in his study, writing all day and all night. Total moodiness. Agony, ecstasy." She lifted her shoulders in a shrug, now sounding tired, almost resigned. "It never ends."

"Guess it's not easy being the kid of a creative genius type." Sam bent to pick up a piece of gnarled driftwood. "Check this out—looks kind of like a dog, doesn't it?"

Charlotte took the driftwood, examined it briefly, then dropped it on the sand. "A dog scratching fleas."

Sam laughed. "You're absolutely right."

"So . . ." Charlotte took a crooked step that caused her to lean closer to Sam. Her bare arm brushed his. "It's obvious Silver Beach is boring with a capital *B*. What do you want to do about it?"

Sam had a feeling he knew what was coming. "We could get a bunch of people together, go into Pentwater tonight," he suggested, his tone neutral. "I heard they twinned their movie theater."

"Two whole choices of second-run films," scoffed Charlotte. "Still in the boring category." She stopped walking and turned toward him, her lashes lowered provocatively. "I was thinking more along the lines of taking that little Mustang of yours for a moonlight drive."

Charlotte smiled up at him, her full lips parted, her eyes warm and deep and inviting.

Sam knew what any other guy in Silver Beach—in the state of Michigan, for that matter—would do at that moment: grab those sexy bare shoulders and kiss her until both their lips were bruised, then get into the Porsche and drive to some romantic, deserted spot. Any other guy. "I don't think so, Char," he said gently.

Charlotte stroked his arm. "Oh, come on," she murmured. "You're not teaching sailing with precious Elli—this is the perfect time to branch out. How do you know you won't like it if you don't try it?"

Sam stifled a sigh. Every summer Charlotte made a play for him, and every summer he put her off. This time he almost found himself feeling sorry for her. "Look, Char," he said. "I have other plans. It's just not going to happen."

She stepped away from him. As her lips tightened in a thin line and her eyes narrowed, her face took on a shuttered look. "I see. Well, okay, Sam DeWitt." She flashed him a smile—disappointed, petulant, but still teasing—then turned on her heel. "Your loss."

He watched her walk back across the dune to Briarwood. The breeze played with her long hair and molded the thin, gauzy skirt to her slender legs. But despite her beautiful, sensual appearance, Sam saw only a willful, needy child. *She's been sleeping around since she was thirteen,* he thought. *But she's still a damned kid.*

He reversed his own course, walking back up past Elli's house. He waved at two shadowy figures sitting on the porch rockers—Ethan and Laura. *No Elli,* he thought with a jolt of disappointment. *And I won't see her later.* They wouldn't bump into each other "accidentally" down on the dock, swim in the warm black water, talk and tell jokes for hours.

A sharp pang of regret pierced his gut. It had been a mistake not to teach sailing with her. Immature. What was he trying to prove? Not that she cared—she hadn't spared a glance or a word for him all day. *Probably pining over that guy back home,* Sam guessed, kicking at a stone.

No, he reminded himself, there were a million and one reasons not to fall for a girl who was so much younger. All of last summer, basically. "No," Sam said out loud, resisting the urge to go back and knock on Elli's door, see if *she* wanted to take a drive in the Mustang convertible. "I won't make that mistake again."

Elli sat on the living room sofa, reading one of the mysteries she'd brought for her summer reading. Her grandmother was flipping through a gardening supplies catalog, murmuring aloud to herself occasionally. "We could use some new hedge clippers—the old ones are so rusty and stiff. And wouldn't this birdbath be sweet over in the corner by the rosebushes?"

Elli looked up from her book and out the window behind the sofa. Lights twinkled in a sea of black: Briarwood, across the broad lawn. A tiny shudder crawled over Elli's skin. Was it her imagination, or did the lights seem to pulse with strange, powerful emotion? *Charlotte's angry, restless,* thought Elli with certainty. *I can feel it.* Then she laughed out loud. Talk about a hyperactive imagination. Maybe Charlotte was bent out of shape, but if it wasn't getting to Ethan, it certainly shouldn't get under her skin.

Mrs. Chapman looked at Elli over the rims of her bifocals, head tipped to one side and a quizzical smile on her softly wrinkled face. "Funny book, dear?"

"I was just thinking about . . . about the Ransoms," Elli replied. Unaccountably her focus shifted from Charlotte. "Mr. Ransom asking Mom out to dinner tonight."

"Hmm." Mrs. Chapman closed the catalog. "Does it strike you as odd?"

Elli shook her head. "Not odd, really. But I always wondered." She wasn't sure how much her grandmother knew about Mr. and Mrs. Wells's last big fight the previous summer, on Midsummer Madness weekend. Right before the blowup, at the costume ball, Elli had been almost one hundred percent certain she'd glimpsed her mother in a clandestine embrace with Mr. Ransom. A measure of the worry she'd experienced then returned now. "I mean, I know they've known each other forever, grew up together, but I've wondered if they were ever . . . more than friends."

"Holling doesn't have many close friends," mused Mrs. Chapman, "but he does appear to confide in Grace. As you said, they grew up together. I believe she was a comfort to him after his wife's unfortunate death."

For a few minutes Elli and her grandmother lapsed back into silence. Then Mrs. Chapman spoke. "The eagles' nest, my dear. Have you been over to Blueberry Island to see it?"

Elli bit her lip. "No. One of these days." *If Sam wants to go with me,* she added silently, *which isn't likely.* She thought about day camp, and his surprising switch from sailing to water-skiing. It could mean only one thing. This summer wasn't going to start out like the one before. They weren't going to be close companions, much less anything else.

"It's not the same, is it, now that it's not your special secret, yours and Sam's," remarked Mrs. Chapman, resuming her casual perusal of the catalog.

Elli blinked, startled. Was her grandmother a mind reader? "I guess not," she mumbled.

A gust of cool evening air stirred the curtain. Mrs. Chapman looked up. "Nice night for a walk or a swim," she observed, rising slowly to her feet. "It's bed for me, though. See you in the morning." She dropped a kiss on Elli's cheek, then crossed to the hallway. Elli heard the door to the master suite close.

Nice night for a walk or a swim. Abruptly Elli stood up and started toward the door. She hesitated, her hand on the knob. Then she turned and headed for the staircase instead. She brushed her teeth and washed her face, then changed into a nightgown and crawled into bed with her book.

Five minutes later she was up again, standing at the window, the curtains pushed aside and her nose close to the screen. The moon was dropping lower in the western sky, laying a trail of silver across the lake. The white sand glowed softly in the dark. The beach was empty.

As she turned away, pulling the curtains closed again, she realized she'd been more than half hoping to see someone out there. Maybe it wasn't Charlotte's restlessness she'd been feeling earlier—maybe it was her own.

3

"Let's meet for lunch," Laura suggested to Elli before heading out the door with Ethan. "Come up to the clubhouse when you're done with sailing, okay?"

"Sounds good," said Elli, spreading jam on a second piece of toast.

"Later, El," said Ethan.

"Have a fun morning," she responded.

The screen door banged shut behind her brother and his girlfriend. Elli munched her toast, idly glancing at the front-page stories in the local paper. Through the open window in the breakfast room, she could hear her grandmother humming as she pottered around in the garden.

Mrs. Wells came in, wearing slippers and a lightweight cotton robe, just as Elli was finishing her breakfast. "Morning," she said.

"You're up early," Elli commented.

Mrs. Wells laughed. "Eight-thirty isn't especially early."

"I mean, considering." Her mother and Mr. Ransom had returned from dinner around eleven, and when Elli had woken up and looked sleepily at her digital clock at two A.M., they were still talking on the porch. "You had kind of a late night."

"You know how it is at the start of the summer, seeing your friends for the first time in almost a year," Mrs. Wells said lightly as she poured herself a cup of coffee at the sideboard. "So much to catch up on."

Friends. Elli raised her juice glass to her lips and studied her mother over the rim. *That wasn't how it looked on the yacht club deck at the Midsummer Madness costume ball,* she thought. But then, she'd never been sure exactly what she'd seen. Had the embrace been passionate, or had her mother just been consoling Mr. Ransom on the anniversary of his wife's death? Mr. Wells, too, had seen his wife with another man, and immediately after had packed his bags and left Silver Beach. But they'd been fighting all summer—all year. Who knew, really, what had cemented their estrangement?

Since her parents had separated, they'd both become happier people, more relaxed and easier to get along with. Elli didn't blame her mother for the separation—it had always been clear that both her parents contributed to the tension, the misunderstandings. But while she and her mom were getting along pretty well these days, they hadn't exactly evolved into friends who were comfortable talking about anything and everything. Elli sensed her mother had secrets. "So, it wasn't a date," Elli ventured at last.

Mrs. Wells poured some cream in her coffee. "Oh, no," she said lightly.

"Because you and Dad are still— I mean—"

Her mother stirred her coffee, then tapped the spoon on the rim. "Holling and I have been friends since childhood, and that's all we are— just very good friends."

Elli nodded. "Yeah, sure, of course. I didn't mean to be— Well, anyway." She pushed back her chair. "I'd better get going. Have a nice day, Mom."

Mrs. Wells reached for the newspaper. "You too, hon."

Elli carried her dishes from the breakfast room to the adjacent kitchen, depositing them in the sink with a clatter. She hoped her mother was listening and picking up the vibes. *Just very good friends—ha.* Elli marched down the hall and out the door to the porch. *I hope she could tell that I could tell that's a lie.*

"Why didn't I stick to tennis?" Charlotte grumbled as she wrestled a capsized Sunfish back into an upright position.

Elli, still dry in her own boat, laughed. "Think how hot and sweaty you'd be, out there on the courts all day," she pointed out. "We get to keep cool, take a dip whenever we want."

"I wouldn't call this taking a dip," Charlotte complained as she hauled Maggie Parker and Stephen Brewster, bobbing in the cove in their bright orange life preservers, back into the boat with her. "Now, were you watching me?" she asked, addressing the two small campers. "Because it's really important that you know how to do that yourselves."

"Right," Elli confirmed, "so let's try it one more time."

"You're kidding," Charlotte groaned.

Elli grinned. "It's really important—you said so yourself."

"Okay, okay," Charlotte agreed reluctantly. "Ten more minutes of capsizing drills. But then we end the day with something fun, right, kids?"

"Right!" asserted a chorus of high-pitched voices.

"Something fun" turned out to be a round-the-cove race. As the kids piloted their Sunfishes in an erratic circle, ropes and sails flapping, Charlotte and Elli jumped up and down on the dock, cheering them on. Miraculously, all five boats made it back to the dock without mishap. "You guys nearly bought it on the other side of the cove," Charlotte said to eight-year-old Casey McAllister and her younger brother, Mitchell. "I thought I was going to have to dive in after you."

"We didn't tip, though," Casey told her proudly.

"Nope, you didn't," Charlotte agreed. "Good job."

The kids discarded their life preservers and galloped up the dock. "See you tomorrow," Elli called after them.

One by one, she and Charlotte hauled the small sailboats up onto the beach. "We should have taught the kids to do this part, too, while we were at it," said Charlotte, huffing.

Elli coiled a length of line over her arm. "Had to save something for tomorrow's lesson." Together, the two girls reefed the sails and then trudged back down the dock to stow the life preservers. "You know," Elli said after a few minutes, "you're really good at this."

"At what?" asked Charlotte, lifting her arms to braid her damp, tangled hair.

"Teaching sailing. Working with kids."

"Funny, seeing as how I can't stand 'em," Charlotte said dryly.

Elli gave Charlotte a thoughtful look. *Oh, no, here it comes,* Charlotte said to herself. *The last thing I need is to be psychoanalyzed by little Miss I'm So Perfect and You're So Flawed.* She knew how to throw Elli off balance—it was something she'd been good at since they were little girls. "So, Eleanor, what did you think about our parents' hot date last night?"

Elli paused in the act of depositing an armful of life jackets in the storage bin. "I didn't think it *was* a hot date."

Charlotte laughed low in her throat. "Well, of course everything's relative. My dad's as cold as they come, so maybe *hot* is the wrong word. But *date* definitely applies. This is the first time he's taken a woman out to dinner since . . . And they went to the Golden Dunes Café in Pentwater— pretty romantic. What's the problem, anyway? Your parents are divorced."

"Separated."

"Same difference. And your mom's gotta keep herself amused somehow, right?"

Elli continued her work, not meeting Charlotte's mocking gaze. "My mother says she and your dad are just . . . Well, I guess it's none of our business."

Charlotte smirked at the thought of all Elli's futile efforts over the years to keep her and Ethan apart. "And you *never* stick your nose into things that aren't your business, do you?" she said, her voice dripping with scorn and sarcasm.

Elli let the lid of the storage bin drop with a loud bang. She was blushing, but she tossed back her hair and looked Charlotte straight in the eye anyway. "Listen, Charlotte. I don't like this camp counseling assignment any better than you do. But we don't have a choice, so we might as well make the best of it. Today went really well—why don't we leave it at that?"

Well, that's a switch, Charlotte thought appreciatively. For once, Elli was being honest instead of prissy and roundabout. Everything about Elli had always been so annoyingly perfect—her family, her whole life. But the myth of the perfect family had been shattered. Maybe Elli was still a golden girl, but the setting in which she'd sparkled had been tarnished, and no amount of polishing was going to bring back the shine. *We're on an even footing,* Charlotte thought, a small measure of the resentment she'd harbored over the years fading. *She can't act so superior anymore.*

"Okay," said Charlotte cheerfully. "I'll keep my claws in if you will."

A ghost of a smile flickered behind Elli's blue eyes. "Deal," she said.

When the movie let out Friday night, the group of Silver Beach teenagers milled about on the sidewalk in front of the Pentwater Cinema. "So, where do you want to go now?" asked Chip Branford.

"There's the usual exciting choices," said Charlotte. "Pizza or ice cream."

Elli shrugged. "Whatever. I don't care."

"The tables at Luigi's are bigger," said Sam. "Let's go there."

The suggestion agreed upon, they all turned and headed down the block to Luigi's. Elli walked alongside her brother and Laura, her eyes fixed on the couple a few steps ahead of her. Sam and Julia. *Are they or aren't they?* she wondered, a sharp, sick feeling tightening in her chest. Sam and Julia had driven to Pentwater together, just the two of them—Julia's younger brother, Chad, had come in another car. And though they weren't holding hands, there was something about the way they kept pace with each other, their arms nearly brushing, that bothered Elli more than she liked to admit.

Ethan dropped back to say something to Hugh and Chad. When he was out of earshot, Laura turned to Elli. "Looks like Chip is the flavor of the day, huh?" she murmured.

Chip had an arm slung around Charlotte's shoulders; Charlotte's hand was tucked in the back pocket of his jeans. "She's been out with a different guy every night this week," Elli agreed with a wry laugh. "That's her signature style, all right."

Ethan caught up again, wedging himself in between them. "What are you two gossiping about?" he asked, wrapping both arms around Laura.

Laura smiled at Elli over Ethan's shoulder. "Oh, nothing," she said innocently.

Elli returned the smile. As Ethan and Laura stopped for a brief kiss, Elli continued on alone, her hands pushed deep in the pockets of her denim jacket.

At Luigi's they crowded around a long table, pulling up extra chairs. Elli sat between Chad and Amelia. As they debated what kind of pizzas to order, she stole glances around the table. *People really seem to be pairing up fast this summer,* she observed. Ethan and Laura, Heather and Hugh, Doug and Amber, Sam and Julia.

"What do you want, El?" asked Chad.

I want Sam DeWitt, she thought with a jolt, then shook her head and peered at the menu. "I don't know. Anything veggie, I guess—I really don't care."

They ordered four large pizzas and a couple of pitchers of soda. Trying not to look at Sam and Julia in conversation at the other end of the table, Elli fiddled with her paper napkin, her plastic straw, her knife and fork. Then abruptly she shoved back her chair. "I'm going to stick some quarters in the jukebox," she announced. "Any requests?"

"Something mellow," said Julia, leaning closer to Sam.

"Something wild," countered Charlotte, running a hand up Chip's arm to the back of his neck.

Elli stalked to the rear of the restaurant. When she reached the jukebox, she realized Chad had followed her. "I have a pocketful of change," he explained, jingling the coins.

51

"Thought I'd make a contribution."

Elli pressed a button, flipping through the CD titles. "What are you in the mood for?" she asked, and instantly her face grew warm. She hadn't meant to sound so flirtatious. Chad rested one arm against the top of the jukebox; they stood close to each other, checking out the selections. "Not Nirvana. Yeah, maybe something mellow. Easier to talk that way."

Elli picked a Gin Blossoms song and another by the Cranberries. "So, I suppose teaching the tennis clinic at camp means you're too tired to play a game for fun at the end of the day," she speculated.

Chad gave her an easy, inviting smile. "Nah. The kids do all the running around—I just stand at the net lobbing balls at them. Why, what did you have in mind?"

"I was thinking in terms of a rematch." Elli returned his smile, noticing for the first time that Chad had gorgeous dark gray eyes. "We played once last summer, remember? You beat me pretty badly. But I worked on my game a lot this past spring."

"I'd love to see you in action," said Chad. "How about tomorrow afternoon?"

"Sounds good."

They walked back to the table, still chatting about tennis. Elli was flirting—she wasn't sure why, but once she'd started, she couldn't seem to stop.

And why shouldn't I? she asked herself. Chad was easygoing, fun, and very good-looking—tall and athletic, with thick red-brown hair and a cute sprinkle of freckles across his nose. She shot a glance at Sam to see if he'd noticed her and Chad at the jukebox, but he was completely absorbed in conversation with Julia. *What am I saving myself for, anyway? If Chad's interested . . .*

Chad *was* interested. For the rest of the meal, he hung on Elli's every word, giving her his exclusive attention. Unlike Sam, who hardly glanced at her the entire evening.

Charlotte placed one hand on Chip's thigh, then pressed herself against him so she could whisper in his ear. "Hurry up and finish your pizza." She gave his earlobe a gentle, teasing nip. "I'm ready to get out of here."

She could feel the tense, eager expectation of Chip's hard, athletic body, and her own body softened responsively. It was an automatic reflex that didn't mean anything. The words and the playful little kisses were a game, and having an audience normally added some spice. But tonight, more than usual, she was just going through the motions. Tonight, a specific audience was more important than the object of her attention, Chip, and that audience wasn't even watching. He couldn't have cared less.

He has to have noticed the way I'm hanging

all over Chip, thought Charlotte, stealing a glance at Ethan out of the corner of her eye. *He has to be jealous—it has to bring back memories that get him right in the gut.*

But Ethan seemed oblivious to the spectacle Charlotte was making of herself. Engaged in an animated conversation at the other end of the table, he sat with one arm draped around Laura's shoulders, his fingers firmly gripping the flesh of Laura's upper arm. *I was the first for him,* thought Charlotte. *He was going to love me forever.* So how could he touch another girl so casually, look into her eyes, bend his head to kiss her, just like that, as if Charlotte didn't even exist anymore? The pain that surged through Charlotte's heart was new and startling: desire magnified with nostalgia and anger; a fierce, vindictive longing.

She'd forgotten Sam and how he'd rejected her once again. That wasn't anything new—it hurt, but it was part of summer. But Ethan had always been hers exclusively. Ethan worshiped the ground she walked on, and it was Charlotte's prerogative to grant him as much or as little attention as she wanted, depending on the mood of the moment. He'd *always* wanted her more than she wanted him—that was the foundation of their relationship. And now the roles had been reversed. As Charlotte stroked Chip Branford's muscular arm she felt herself burning up inside from wanting Ethan so badly, wanting him more with every passing moment that she was forced to watch him and Laura blissfully happy together.

"They are just so *happy*," she murmured to Chip, the word bitter as poison on the back of her tongue. "Don't they make you sick?"

"They're saps," Chip agreed in a low voice. "They deserve each other." His hand slipped around Charlotte's waist, under her shirt. "Wells never deserved *you,* that's for sure."

Chip's fingers inched up toward her ribs and Charlotte shivered slightly, but not with pleasure. Ethan's happiness, a happiness she couldn't share, was a knife twisting deeper in her heart. The only way to end the pain, she knew, was to take that beautiful, despised happiness and break it into a million pieces.

"Rasta, come on, boy," Ethan called out at home later that night. "Let's go get some air, stretch our legs."

The retriever bounded to the door, tail wagging joyfully. Ethan pushed open the door and Rasta took off across the lawn like a bullet, melting into the darkness. Ethan followed the sound of the dog's jingling collar, his sneakers immediately soaked by the dewy grass.

Rasta snuffled around in the bank of weeds and wildflowers that separated the lawn from the beach, then galloped down to the sand. When he reached the beach himself, Ethan slowed to a stop and gazed up at the stars. The night was so beautiful, so peaceful—the silence so pure. And he felt relaxed, at ease, in a way he never had before at Silver Beach. *Because Laura's the center now, not Charlotte,* Ethan thought, glancing over his shoulder at Briarwood, where a light burned behind the curtain in Charlotte's window. Charlotte was like a comet blazing across the sky, but Laura was the north star, steady and bright. He just had to keep his eyes fixed on that star.

He was still looking at Charlotte's window when a voice spoke out of the shadows behind him. "I'm not there," the voice whispered, "I'm here."

Ethan spun around, drawing in his breath sharply. Charlotte stood just a few feet away, her face and her golden hair pale in the moonlight. "Oh, Char, it's you. You nearly gave me a heart attack."

"Sorry. I didn't mean to scare you. But I was taking a walk, and when I saw you . . . I knew I shouldn't, but I couldn't help myself."

She stepped closer, and Ethan's body tensed defensively. He wrapped himself mentally in armor. "Charlotte, don't," he said as she gripped his arm.

Her eyes sparkled with tears. "How could you?" she asked, her voice breaking. "How could you break my heart like this?"

Ethan gave an aborted laugh. "*I'm* breaking

your heart? Come on, Char. You know it was always the other way around." A pained note entered his voice. "You're the one who cheated on *me.* And what was I supposed to think when you didn't answer any of my letters?"

"I've just been so busy," Charlotte protested. "You have no idea how much work they give us at Branford Hall. It didn't mean I wasn't thinking about you. I still cared. I still—"

"Admit it, Char," Ethan cut in. "If you cared, you wouldn't have blown me off. Your heart can't be broken—it's much too hard."

She shook her head vehemently. "You think I can't feel pain? Well, you're wrong. Seeing you with her . . . it hurts me more than anything ever has."

"I'm sorry," said Ethan. "I'm just . . . sorry."

They stood silently for a moment in the dark. Then Charlotte blurted out, "You can't love her, Ethan. You just can't. Don't you remember what you said to me last summer, how we were born to love each other, how we'd always been a part of each other and always would be? Inevitable, that's what you said. Forever."

"And I believed it then, but you didn't," Ethan countered. "I *did* love you, Char, with all my heart, but it was never enough for you. Don't you remember that part?"

She stared at him through a wild tangle of hair. "I only remember us being together, how good it felt, better than with anyone else. Admit it, Ethan. It *was* better. You remember, too, I know you do."

She was so close now, he could feel the heat of her body, smell the sensuous, musky jasmine scent of her skin and hair, see the solitary tear creeping down her cheek. He placed his hands on her shoulders, but only so he could hold her at arm's length. "I remember that you lied to me, that you cheated on me with Sloan Hammond," said Ethan, his voice calm and passionless. "And I always went crawling back to you—that was my own fault. But I don't have to crawl anymore. I've learned that's not what love is about."

"I don't want you to crawl," said Charlotte. "I just want—"

Her face was tipped up to his, her lips parted. A year earlier, Ethan would have gone to her unhesitatingly and devoured those lips, kissing her until his identity dissolved and melted into hers. *Because I was a crazy, insecure, inexperienced, lovesick kid,* he thought. *I didn't know my own name when I was around her.*

Now he was stronger—so much stronger, in fact, that he didn't even feel tempted. He stepped back from her, dropping his hands from her arms. "Good night, Charlotte."

She shrank away from him, into herself, her arms folded across her chest and her face hidden behind a curtain of hair. For a second she hesitated, and then whirled and ran off across the dunes without speaking. With a sigh of relief, Ethan whistled for Rasta and turned back toward the cottage. Inside, he closed the door behind him and leaned against it for a moment. Then he walked quietly up the stairs to Laura.

4

Charlotte woke to the sound of a car in the driveway. She sat up in bed and leaned over to the window, nudging the curtain aside with her index finger. Her father's Mercedes was parked below, the powerful engine idling. There were two people in the front seat, but in the faint pink light of dawn, it was impossible to see them clearly. Did they bend toward each other, exchange a quick kiss? She couldn't tell.

The passenger door swung open and a woman stepped out of the car. Grace Wells tossed Charlotte's father a good-bye wave, then hurried across the lawn, disappearing into her own house. Charlotte sank back against the pillows on her bed. A wave of nausea washed suddenly over her—she almost felt like vomiting. Then the feeling passed and she scowled. *Out together all night. They* are *having an affair,* she deduced.

Imagine that, Dad actually paying attention to something besides his damned writing. Dad dating! And dating for the first time since Mrs. Ransom's death—Charlotte was intensely aware of this striking fact. Dating Mrs. Wells.

Charlotte looked out the window again, but her father must have already entered the house. Before her, Silver Beach lay sleeping in the early dawn. There was no movement except that of the grass and the water and the trees, no sign that two middle-aged people had just sneaked back into the colony after a night of illicit love.

She stared at the Chapman cottage, and it stared back at her. The driveway—that very spot on the driveway evoked for her the day of her mother's death. It had been August, Midsummer Madness weekend, and Charlotte had been eight years old. She'd found her mother's lifeless body bobbing face down in the shallow waters of the cove and, galvanized by terror, had run for her father. He had been standing in the Chapmans' driveway. She could almost see him—younger, his hair blacker. He'd been laughing—she remembered that best of all because it had given his face a happy, affectionate expression she so rarely saw herself. He'd been laughing as he showed Elli Wells how to work the gears on her new ten-speed and chatting, so easily and jovially, with Elli's mother. *Like Elli didn't already have a father, like Grace didn't already*

61

have a husband, thought Charlotte resentfully. *Like he didn't have a wife and daughter of his own.* Laughing—while Annette Ransom, desperate and alone, took her own life.

Charlotte remembered how, the other day at camp, she had ribbed Elli about their parents dating. Teased her, as though their date was a big joke, as though it couldn't possibly amount to anything. But now, unable to shake the image of her father and Mrs. Wells parting in the driveway at dawn, Charlotte felt her skin crawl.

She sat at the window for a long while. Finally, in the east, the sun edged up over the treetops, bathing the colony in a bright yellow glow. Charlotte wrapped herself in a thick white terrycloth bathrobe and padded downstairs to the kitchen. Mr. Ransom had just flipped a couple of fried eggs onto a plate and was about to stick the frying pan in the sink. "Leave it on the stove," Charlotte requested. "I think I'll have eggs, too."

He did as she asked, without speaking. Charlotte turned the heat back up under the skillet and cracked open two eggs. While the eggs sizzled, she leaned back against the counter with her weight on one foot, one ankle crossed over the other. Breakfast together on a sunny summer morning—a perfect time for a lighthearted father-daughter chat. *Talk,* Charlotte instructed herself. *Somebody has to start the ball rolling.*

"So . . ." She wanted to ask about his date with Mrs. Wells, but she knew from long experience that it was better to be cautious, impersonal. If he heard the faintest trace of emotion in her voice, he'd freeze her out completely. "Anything interesting in the newspaper?"

Mr. Ransom riffled through the pages. "The usual north country excitement," he said blandly. "Deer struck by auto. Auto struck by deer. Local minister runs off with church choir director. Mrs. Mulligan's cat rescued from tree."

Charlotte laughed. "Don't you miss New York sometimes?"

"Sometimes," her father replied.

He sopped up some egg yolk with a piece of toast, his eyes on the paper. Charlotte waited for him to say something—ask if she had any special plans for the day, how camp counseling was going. She waited for a long minute even though she knew no cheerful fatherly questions were coming. Then she turned back to the skillet.

By the time her own breakfast was ready, her father was placing his plate in the dishwasher and refilling his coffee cup in preparation for his retreat to his study. *I could do what I did last summer,* Charlotte thought, remembering the terrible scene when she'd shouted at her father, for the first time in her life confronting him with her suspicion that her mother had killed herself rather than drowned accidentally. He'd slapped

her, both with his hand and with a lash of stinging words, but at least for a moment there'd
been *feeling* between them. Hating was better
than not caring. But a year later, her father was
once again treating her like a stranger: tolerating
her while barely acknowledging her existence,
his manner unfailingly civil, disinterested, cold.
The accusations, the revelations, hadn't brought
them closer—there was still a wall between
them, stony and forbidding.

And her consolation—Ethan—was gone. Alone
at the kitchen table, Charlotte pierced her egg
with a fork, watching the yolk run across the plate
like blood. She'd wasted her time on the beach
the previous night—his power of resistance had
taken her by surprise. *But I know you, Ethan
Wells,* Charlotte thought, tearing a piece of toast
into bits, *better than you know yourself.* She'd adjust her strategy, refine it. Then they'd see how
long Ethan could hold out.

"I used to ride my bike over here with my
friend Sally Hammond," Elli told Laura one
breezy afternoon as they pedaled along the road
that led past the Jantzens' farm. "We picked
berries."

"Sally—she's the one whose family moved
downstate this past winter. The local girl, right?"

"Right," said Elli. "And her brother Sloan was
the one who . . . well, you know. That thing with

Charlotte last summer. Anyway, it's pretty over here, isn't it? I mean, the lake isn't the only nice thing about northern Michigan."

On the shoulder of the road just beyond the farmstand, they leaned their bikes against some trees. "There's a nice path through the woods and over this really pretty meadow," Elli continued. "We'll end up at the farm and pick some strawberries. How does that sound?"

"Perfect," said Laura, taking a deep breath of the fresh country air.

They strolled along the mossy, sun-dappled path, their arms swinging. "I miss Sally, actually," Elli confessed. "I mean, we had some problems last summer, but she was a close friend. There aren't really any other girls at Silver Beach that I like as much. That's one reason it's nice having you here this summer."

Laura smiled. "I feel lucky that Ethan has such a great family. I mean, I get along better with you than I do with my own sisters."

Elli laughed. "Well, you're like the sister I never had."

Laura bent to examine some lilies of the valley growing at the roots of a mossy old beech tree. "I'm just having so much *fun*. This could have been a washout, you know? Spending so much time together—Ethan and I might have found out that we didn't have as much in common as we thought, gotten bored. But it's not happening that way."

"I'm glad," said Elli sincerely.

"I'll admit I was secretly worried at first, though," said Laura with a wry laugh. "Just a little, about Charlotte. It was one thing hearing about her back in Winnetka, but to actually see her, to be living right next door to her, is another story. And she's gorgeous."

"She is," agreed Elli. "But if anyone ever proved the maxim that beauty's only skin deep, it's Charlotte!"

"We haven't actually had a conversation, she and I," said Laura. "Is she that bad? Is it absolutely awful being paired up with her at camp?"

"Not as bad as I thought it would be," said Elli, squinting against the bright sunlight as they emerged from the woods into the meadow. "In a weird way, we have sort of complementary personalities. I think I'm better at making sure the kids actually learn something, but Char's just got this charisma. She makes the kids laugh, lets them get silly. They all have a crush on her, boys *and* girls."

"So she can be nice when she wants to," remarked Laura.

"When she wants to," Elli emphasized. "I'm glad she's not making it hard for you and Ethan. I mean, she could. She's the Queen of the Scene, the Mistress of Melodrama."

Laura laughed. "She really has backed off. There are so many guys after her—I guess she's realized she doesn't need Ethan."

Maybe Charlotte's backed off, but don't bet on her staying that way. Elli opened her mouth to say something to that effect, then closed it again, swallowing the comment. Why not look at the bright side? Maybe Laura was right. Maybe Charlotte had finally learned her lesson and was going to keep her distance.

"So, speaking of crushes," said Laura, "tell me about Sam DeWitt."

Elli raised her eyebrows. "Sam?"

"Oh, come on," Laura chided, smiling. "I can tell you have a thing for him."

"I don't have a thing for him," Elli protested, feeling her face grow warm. "I mean, okay, I did when I was younger, when he was my sailing instructor. All the girls did."

"And now?" Laura probed.

Elli shrugged. "Last year we entered the Midsummer Madness regatta in his grandfather's yacht, the *Silver Dollar,* and we won. But this year he asked Julia to race with him." Elli couldn't mask the hurt in her voice. "There's not much point having a crush on him, seeing as how he's going out with someone else."

"Hmm," murmured Laura thoughtfully. "Will you enter the regatta anyway?"

Elli shook her head. "Chad asked me to play

in the doubles tennis tournament with him. I guess I'll focus on that."

The path had looped back to the road and the farmstand. Baskets in hand, Elli and Laura wandered over to the strawberry field. "So, the day camp writing program is really going well," Laura chattered. "Even better than I hoped. The kids have the funniest ideas for plays."

"Like what?" asked Elli.

Laura began cheerfully describing the plays, but Elli couldn't really focus—all she could think about was Sam. She knew it would be fun practicing for the tournament with Chad, but she also knew it wouldn't hold a candle to training for the regatta with Sam. All those wonderful hours out on the open lake, the magic of their teamwork—and the regatta itself, the thrilling victory, the award ceremony, the dance that night at the yacht club, the kiss.

Elli shook away the memory. *Our names are engraved on the silver cup—big deal.* It looked as though that was all that was left, as though that was all that was going to last.

"So, in Antonia and Casey's play we have five main speaking parts," said Laura to the campers sitting in a circle around her. "There's an eight-year-old girl named Miranda, her older brother, Tommy, their parents, and the family dog, Leopold, who seems to talk as much as anybody. Who wants to play the dog?"

Every hand shot into the air and the room erupted in shouts of "Me, me, me!"

Ethan laughed. "That settles it," he joked, grinning at Laura. "Next play *I* write, *all* the characters are going to be canines."

They cast the play and read through the short script twice. Predictably, Leopold got lots of laughs. When the hour was through, Ethan and Laura walked the campers to the door of the clubhouse. "Remember, tonight you're all supposed to raid your attics," Laura instructed them. "We decided to set *A Rainy Day at the Beach* back in the old days at the beginning of the twentieth century, so we're looking for those funny-looking old-fashioned bathing suits and any other odds and ends your grandparents don't mind you playing with."

The kids marched out of the clubhouse, a few of them shouting out their lines at the tops of their lungs. "How about something to eat?" Ethan suggested to Laura.

"Sounds good," she replied. "I'm ravenous."

"How about getting something here instead of going back to the house?"

Laura agreed, and they ordered burgers and fries at the yacht club grill, then took their food out onto the deck. "I like this spot," said Laura, gesturing broadly. "You can see the whole colony.

Everybody puttering on their boats, the golfers coming in after a morning on the links, people mowing their lawns and clipping their hedges. It's like having front-row seats at the theater."

"This place is kind of like a fishbowl," Ethan agreed, dunking a french fry in some ketchup. "It's hard not to know what everyone else is up to."

Down below, two girls were walking up the dock. Elli looked up, saw them, and waved. Ethan and Laura waved back. Charlotte, however, didn't so much as glance in their direction. "She's ignoring you, huh?" observed Laura. "I'm sorry you two couldn't just be friends."

Ethan tore his eyes away from Charlotte. "It's better this way," he mumbled through a big bite of hamburger. He thought about the encounter on the beach the other night and hoped Laura couldn't read his mind—he hadn't told her about it. Charlotte *had* been ignoring him since then, and he wasn't sure if he was relieved or disappointed. "I mean, being friends after you break up—how often does that really happen? Anyway, Charlotte doesn't have guy friends. Either you're her totally adoring sex slave or you're a stranger. There's no in between."

Laura laughed. "I just can't imagine being that kind of girl."

"That's because you're the exact opposite."

"Boring, you mean," said Laura with a wry smile. "Tame. Predictable."

"No." Ethan put a hand on top of hers. "Sweet, wonderful, thoughtful." He lowered his voice to a whisper. "And, might I add, totally hot."

She shook her head, a faint blush tingeing her smooth cheeks. "What am I going to do with you, Ethan Wells?" she asked with pretend exasperation.

"Whatever you want," replied Ethan with a smile.

A minute later, Elli joined them. The three ate lunch together, idly talking and laughing. At one point, Laura ducked inside to go to the restroom.

Ethan glanced at his sister. "I'm seeing you a lot more this summer," he observed.

"Yeah, I've noticed that, too," Elli replied.

"It's because of Laura, right?" Ethan guessed. "I mean, face it, we wouldn't have been sitting here like this last year, when I was going out with Charlotte."

Elli laughed. "Probably not."

"So much is different about this summer." Ethan leaned back in his seat, his arms spread along the deck railing. "I mean, all of Silver Beach feels different to me."

"Without Charlotte in the middle."

Ethan nodded. Without Charlotte in the middle, alternately causing him incredible pain and delirious joy; without Charlotte literally shaping him with her hands into a new person, taking him places he hadn't known existed, then abandoning him. *Don't forget that part,* Ethan prompted himself. "It's better now," he said aloud.

"Good," said Elli, biting into her club sandwich.

Laura returned, sliding onto the bench next to him. He felt her hand on his knee; she squeezed gently. Ethan smiled at her, allowing his gaze to linger for a long, appreciative moment on her face, the sweet sparkling eyes, the warm curve of her generous smile. *It's better now,* he thought. *This is the way it should be.* Maybe he wasn't overcome by passion when he was with Laura, but that was because they had something deeper, more solid and dependable. The physical attraction was there, sure, but also affection, fidelity, trust: friendship, plain and simple. *It's better,* he repeated silently, firmly, wondering why he had to work so hard to convince himself. *It's better.*

Elli waded into the cove, drawing the kayak into the water beside her. She was just about to step in when someone called out behind her. "Where you headed, Wells?"

She turned, putting a hand to her forehead to shield her eyes from the afternoon sun. "Oh, hi, Sam." She cleared her throat, stalling for time. How could she tell him she was planning to visit the eagles' nest on Blueberry Island, to see if the eggs had hatched yet and to mope about the intimacy she no longer shared with him? "I was just going for a little paddle. In the cove."

Sam stepped up to the water's edge. "Bag the kayak and I'll take you out on the *Dollar*," he offered, gesturing to his grandfather's boat, moored to a buoy in the cove. "The breeze is picking up."

The breeze *was* picking up; it ruffled Elli's hair and caressed her skin with an almost irresistible invitation. What she wouldn't give to be out on the lake at the helm of a boat as sleek and fast as the *Silver Dollar* again, with Sam. And was there an equally warm invitation in Sam's eyes? "It'll be like the old days," he urged. "Come on."

The old days, Elli repeated to herself. *But it won't be like the old days, because we're not training for the regatta. You picked someone else over me. Well, thanks anyway, but I don't need you to do me any favors. I'm not that desperate.* "Actually, I only have about fifteen minutes," she said, taking a step backward. "Then I have somewhere else to be."

"Maybe another time, then," said Sam.

Elli shrugged. "Maybe."

She settled into the kayak and pushed off from the shallows with her paddle. Without looking back, she could picture Sam walking up the lawn to the clubhouse, hands in the pockets of his baggy khaki shorts and his eyes peeled for Julia. She bit her lip, dipping the paddle and having second thoughts. *Maybe I just cut off my nose to spite my face. It might have been fun. It might have been—*

No. She shook back her hair defiantly. She didn't need the crumbs from Sam DeWitt's table. Besides, she did have someplace else to be later that afternoon. She had a date. With Chad Emerson.

"Oh, I'm a horrible bowler," groaned Elli, laughing as she sank another gutter ball. "Why did we come here?"

"Because this is the only sport I can beat you at," said Chad, grinning. He swung and released his ball, watching as it rolled cleanly down the center of the lane. "Strike!"

Elli stuck her tongue out at him. "I hope this is making you feel good."

"It is," he replied. "See, I'm still smarting from losing to you at tennis the other day."

"You let me win," Elli accused good-naturedly. "I could tell you weren't giving me your toughest shots."

"No way—I was playing all out," Chad insisted. "All right, one more game. Double or nothing."

She tilted her head to one side. "I didn't realize we had a bet going."

"Loser buys the ice cream," he said with a grin.

Half an hour later, they strolled down the quiet

sidewalk of the main street in Deep River, double-dip cones in hand. "I think we've done just about everything there is to do in this hick town," remarked Chad. "Movie, bowling, ice cream."

"It's almost a shame not to have a curfew, since the nightlife around here is so stimulating," Elli agreed.

"Your folks don't care when you get in?"

"My grandmother doesn't, and my mom's—actually, she's out tonight herself." *And she'll probably stay out later than me!* Elli thought. "With Charlotte's dad," she added hesitantly, figuring that Chad, along with everyone else in Silver Beach, had by now picked up on the fact that something was going on between her mother and Mr. Ransom.

Chad didn't ask any nosy questions. His thoughts were obviously running on another track. "So there's no hurry to get you back, then. And as it turns out, there's no one home at my house." He shot a shy, hopeful glance at her. "We could watch a video or something."

"Sure," said Elli easily. "Fine with me."

Back in Silver Beach, they sat through a terrible action movie, sharing a bowl of popcorn. Then Chad walked Elli back to her cottage, and they stood for a few minutes on the shadowy porch, talking in hushed voices. "Thanks for coming out tonight," said Chad. "I had a lot of fun."

"Me too," Elli said, meaning it.

75

"So—maybe we could do it again sometime," he ventured. "There's a new seafood restaurant in Pentwater that's supposed to be good."

Elli smiled. "I'm up for it."

Chad took a step away, hesitated, and stepped back toward her. He put a hand on her arm, and Elli turned toward him encouragingly. The kiss was long, gentle, and distinctly pleasurable. *Even better than with Josh,* Elli found herself thinking. She also couldn't help thinking how much better she'd gotten at this dating thing. A year earlier she'd never even been kissed—she hadn't known what to do or say when she was alone with a guy she liked. Now that she had confidence and some experience, the whole thing came almost naturally.

Pulling back, Elli smiled up at Chad in the dark. "See you tomorrow," she whispered.

He brushed her cheek lightly with the back of his hand. "'Night, Elli."

Inside the house, Elli closed the door quietly, then leaned back against it pensively. No doubt about it, spending an evening with Chad hadn't exactly been a chore, and kissing him felt good. But she was just as clear on something else: the reason the whole date had been easy was because she didn't really care one way or another where it led. *No sparks,* Elli thought with a deep, regretful sigh. *No sparks*

76

at all. The kiss hadn't raised her body temperature a single degree—it hadn't turned her upside down and inside out the way a kiss was supposed to, the way that very first kiss of her lifetime had. Her first, last, and only kiss with Sam.

5

"I think Sarah's ready to go on one ski," Julia remarked, taking Sam's hand. They were walking down to the boathouse together before the day's water-skiing lessons. "And the water's nice and calm today. What do you say?"

He swung her hand lightly. "Sarah? Sure. Not Drew, though. Let's build up his confidence a little more."

He and Julia were still holding hands when he spotted Elli on the dock. Instinctively he dropped Julia's hand, but Elli had been looking right at them. She lowered her eyes and turned away. "Why don't you get the boat ready and I'll go grab some life preservers, okay?" Sam said to Julia.

Julia didn't appear to have noticed Elli, or Sam's response to Elli. "Okay," she assented.

Sam caught up to Elli on the dock by the

storage bin. "How's it going?" he asked.

Elli bent over to rummage through the bin. "Good. How 'bout you?"

"Pretty good. But I— Well, to tell you the truth, water-skiing's fun but I kind of miss sailing. I mean . . . I miss sailing with you."

Elli straightened, lifting a hand to push the hair back from her forehead. "You do?" she said, her eyes wide with surprise.

"Well, yeah. We had a good time, didn't we?"

"Yeah," said Elli. "We had a good time."

She straightened up, a baggy day camp T-shirt draping her curves. The sun picked out bright chestnut highlights in her hair, and her lowered lashes cast shadows on her sun-bronzed cheeks. Without even trying, she was so beautiful, so natural—it was all Sam could do not to stare. *And last summer we were close,* he thought. *This girl and I. Practically best friends.* Elli stepped closer to him, her lips curved in a smile, and hope rose in Sam's heart. Maybe she wasn't that serious about that Josh guy back in Winnetka. Maybe it was worth another try.

"You know, Julia and I . . ." Sam gestured vaguely toward the beach. "It's not necessarily— I mean, we're hanging out a lot together, but it's kind of really just because—"

Sam broke off at the sound of footsteps pounding down the dock behind them. In the next instant, Chad Emerson was at their side, wearing court shoes and tennis whites, a couple of rackets tucked under his arm. "Hey, Sam," said Chad with an easy smile. "Elli, glad I caught you before you headed out. Are you still up for tennis this afternoon? Doug and Amber want to take us on."

"Of course," said Elli, turning from Sam to Chad. "We should play every day if it doesn't rain, don't you think? If we really want to win the tournament, that is."

"Sounds good to me," said Chad, slipping an arm around Elli's waist. "So . . . later."

He bent his head and brushed her cheek with a kiss. Elli shot a quick glance at Sam, blushing and laughing. Sam felt something tighten in his chest. He pivoted on his heel, hoping he looked casual. "See ya, guys," he said.

"Bye, Sam," said Elli.

Sam strode back up the dock, his eyes fixed on Julia and the first-hour water-skiing campers who were waiting for him. He repeated Elli's words to himself: *Bye, Sam.* Not another word, not a single hint that she wanted to continue their interrupted conversation.

At the last moment he remembered the life jackets, and doubled back to the storage bin. Elli and Chad were still talking and joking together, their manner warm and familiar. *They look like a couple,* Sam thought. *Guess they are a couple.*

He might as well face it. Julia wasn't the obstacle here, or even that guy back home in Winnetka. He'd imagined the spark in Elli's eyes just a minute before. She'd started up with somebody else. *She's not into you,* Sam concluded, clenching his jaw. *If she ever was. So get over it, buddy. Get over it.*

At midday Elli had lunch on the yacht club lawn with a bunch of other counselors—Ethan, Laura, Chad, Becky, Heather, and Hugh.

"I really want to blow off camp this afternoon," said Heather, lying back on the grass with her head pillowed on Hugh's lap. "Work on my tan."

"I thought that's all you *did,* being a lifeguard—work on your tan," Hugh teased.

"For your information, it's a position of great responsibility," Heather shot back, "because thanks to crummy swimming instructors like you, half these kids don't even know how to doggie-paddle."

Hugh laughed. "Ouch. Did you hear that, Becky? She called us crummy."

Becky plucked a handful of grass and threw it at Heather. "Yeah, somebody's developed an attitude, sitting up there on that tall chair all day, swinging her whistle."

Elli laughed along with the others, very aware of Chad sitting cross-legged next to her, his knee touching hers. She wasn't quite sure how it had happened—they'd had only one official date—but all of a sudden she felt as though they were wearing labels identifying them as boyfriend and girlfriend.

Heather sat up and started plucking grapes from a large green bunch. "So, Elli," she said with a sly smile. "What's the dirt?"

Elli darted an embarrassed glance at Chad. "The dirt? What do you mean?"

"I mean your mom and Mr. Ransom," said Heather. "They're, like, *dating,* aren't they? I think that's absolutely wild."

Elli met her brother's eye. Ethan's mouth was set in a firm line; obviously he didn't feel like gossiping about his own mother. "Yeah, they're dating," she confirmed in a case-closed tone.

Taking a hint had never been Heather's specialty. "How romantic," she said, leaning against Hugh, who obligingly wrapped a muscular arm around her. "Charlotte's father is just such a romantic figure, don't you think? A tragic figure. Alone all these years, and now the girl next door . . ."

Hugh cleared his throat softly.

Heather raised her eyebrows. "What?" she asked, twisting to look at Hugh. "Did I say something wrong?"

"Sometimes you just talk too much," Hugh replied dryly.

"Well, *sorry,*" Heather said to Elli. "I really

didn't think it was such a sensitive subject. I mean, it's not as if everybody doesn't *know.* And it's not as if it's an affair, because your parents are divorced, right?"

Elli balled up her sandwich wrapper and got to her feet. "Don't worry about it, Heather," she said in her most neutral tone, not answering the last question. "See you guys later."

She hadn't gotten far when Ethan called out to her. "El—wait up."

Elli paused until he fell into stride beside her. She didn't have to ask what he was thinking. "Weird, huh?" she commented. "Hearing people talk about Mom and Mr. Ransom like that. So casual. And just the fact that she's *dating* someone." She laughed uneasily. "Mom's married. She was supposed to be done with dating a zillion years ago."

"They're not really married anymore," Ethan pointed out. "I mean, that part doesn't bother me. Dad probably dates people in Chicago—we just don't know about it."

Elli sighed. "I really don't want to think about it."

"Well, what gets to me—what I can't help thinking about," Ethan went on, "is last summer. Before everything fell apart for good between Mom and Dad. Midsummer Madness. Remember? What you told me you thought you saw?"

Elli wasn't in much danger of forgetting. "They were together, Mom and Mr. Ransom. I wasn't sure, though, if they were . . . kissing or anything. And later Mom said—"

"Mom said it didn't mean anything, they were just old friends," Ethan interrupted. "Yeah, and she was *still* saying that a couple of days ago. So the question is, was it *ever* true?"

Elli stopped in her tracks and Ethan did the same. They looked hard at each other. "She's our mother," Elli said in a low, shaky voice. "Don't we have to give her the benefit of the doubt?"

Ethan shrugged. "Yeah, I guess we should."

Elli gestured toward the dock. "Look, I really have to go."

He nodded. "Right. Me too. Catch you later."

Her brother jogged back to the clubhouse. For a moment Elli stared after him. When she turned to face the water, she wasn't seeing it. Instead, other remembered images—some sharp, some fuzzy—flashed before her eyes: Mrs. Wells and Mr. Ransom embracing under the moonlight at the Midsummer Madness costume ball, Mr. Wells appearing on the deck, tears in his eyes—he too had seen his wife with Holling Ransom. *And Charlotte—why am I thinking of Charlotte?* Elli wondered, confused. Charlotte as a little girl of about eight years old. Charlotte's face as she ran up to the Chapman cottage. Elli had been straddling her brand-new bicycle, one foot on a pedal and one on the ground. *And Mom and Mr. Ransom again, talking about*

*something I couldn't hear and wouldn't have un-
derstood, laughing.*

Elli shook her head. The two moments in
time didn't have anything to do with each
other. She was just trying to distract herself
from the current situation. From the fact that
her mother was carrying on an affair with
Charlotte Ransom's father—and that the whole
colony was talking about it.

"Hey, Char, wait up," Ethan called out, strid-
ing across the lawn toward the cove.

After camp, Laura had headed back to the
cottage to change into a bathing suit while
Ethan made an excuse to stop by the dock, sup-
posedly to give a message to Elli. Charlotte
waited as he requested.

"What's up?" she asked coolly.

"Nothing," said Ethan with an awkward
shrug. "I just haven't seen you around much
lately. We never get to . . . you know, just talk."

Charlotte met his eyes, but only for an instant. Then her gaze roved restlessly over the
landscape. "Look, I'm on my way somewhere,
okay? I have plans." Suddenly her expression
brightened. "Be right there!" she called to someone behind Ethan.

Ethan turned to see Tim Courtland waving to
Charlotte from the clubhouse parking lot, a ray
of sunlight reflecting off the car keys he held in

his hand. "See you around," said Charlotte carelessly as she brushed past Ethan.

"Yeah, see you around," he echoed.

Charlotte dashed off, the breeze billowing her honey-blond hair. Ethan sauntered in the opposite direction, making a point of not looking back over his shoulder to see how Charlotte greeted Tim once she was up close. He could imagine it, though. They'd wrap their arms around each other and kiss. Kiss for a long time. Then hop in Tim's white Miata and—

"Boo."

Ethan jumped. Elli had come up behind him. "Man, you scared me," he exclaimed.

"Why?" she asked. "Because I caught you talking to Charlotte?"

"I wasn't really talking to Charlotte," Ethan defended himself. "I mean, I would have, sure, if she'd stuck around. But she's, well . . ."

An engine started back in the parking lot. Elli watched the Miata buzz off in a cloud of dust. "She's being Charlotte," she said, finishing Ethan's sentence. "Does it bother you? I mean, now that you two are history, do you really care what she does?"

"No, of course not," Ethan said, a little too quickly. They started to walk toward the cottage. "I don't care who Char goes out with. But does she have to go out with a different guy practically every night?" Already that summer she'd had flings with Forrest Madden, Chip Branford, Jack Nichols, and now Tim. And that was just Silver Beach—she knew plenty of boys in neighboring towns.

"Like I said, she's just being Charlotte," Elli repeated.

"I worry about her, is all," Ethan reasoned, still feeling as if he had to make an excuse. "She could be upset, too. I mean, about this thing between Mom and her dad. And, yeah, okay, maybe I miss our old friendship. *Just* the friendship part," he added emphatically.

Elli looked at him intently. "Yeah, of *course* just the friendship part."

Ethan had a sickening feeling that he'd just given something away. "Give me some credit, okay, Elli?" he said defensively.

She lifted her hands, palms up. "What did I say?"

"Nothing." He shook his head. "You didn't say anything. I just know that when it comes to me and Charlotte, you always think the worst."

"But I don't have to think the worst, because there is no 'you and Charlotte' anymore," said Elli. "Isn't that the point here?"

"Yeah, I guess it is," agreed Ethan as he climbed up the porch steps to their house. "Laura and I are going to the beach. Feel like swimming?"

"I'm driving into town with Nana. Any requests from the video store?"

"An action movie. Or horror," Ethan suggested before dashing up the stairs.

He made it to Laura's room and knocked on her door. "I'm almost ready," she called. "Be right out."

"Take your time. I still have to change."

When he reached his own room, Ethan suddenly felt a tightness in his chest, his windpipe closing. He sat on the edge of the bed, trying to keep his breathing slow and steady. *How long has it been since I had an asthma attack?* he thought, fumbling for the desk drawer where he'd stuck his inhaler. He yanked open the drawer and clutched the inhaler, his breathing faster but still under control.

Thirty seconds passed, a minute, two, and the attack didn't materialize. He didn't need the inhaler after all. Ethan exhaled, relieved. "Man, what brought that on?" he mumbled to himself, tossing the medication back in the desk. Sometimes it was nothing physical, just stress.

He was about to slam the desk drawer shut when a small white box shoved far to the back caught his eye. He hesitated, then removed the box, holding it in the palm of his hand for a moment before opening it. Inside, a silver ring set with a small opal was nestled on a bed of cotton. Ethan stared at the ring, memories washing over him. He'd bought it at a jewelry store in Pentwater almost a year before, intending to give it to Charlotte when they said good-bye for the summer. Only they'd never actually said good-bye, because Charlotte had left without telling him she was going. They'd made up after the thing with Sloan—at least, Ethan had thought they had. He'd thought Charlotte was still his, still loved him best. *But she was never mine,* he reflected, surprised by the bitterness he still felt. *She never really loved me.*

Then another memory assaulted him, recent and hot. Charlotte on the beach the other night, beautiful, wild, tearful as she accused him of betraying and abandoning her. She'd pushed all the old buttons—or tried to push them, anyway. *We've always been a part of each other and always will be,* he said silently, repeating her words. Words he himself had said, had believed so strongly, only a year before.

I don't feel it anymore, Ethan told himself firmly, replacing the lid of the box. Charlotte was the past, and the ring was just a piece of metal with nothing attached to it—no meaning, no emotion. Maybe he should give it to Laura. *That's what I'll do,* Ethan decided. It would be like an exorcism, proof that he wasn't hiding anything, that he wasn't saving anything—no part of himself, not even the tiniest—for Charlotte.

Standing up, Ethan started to slip the box into the pocket of his shorts. Then, instead, he watched his hand put the box back into the desk drawer—watched as if his hand belonged to someone else. He couldn't or wouldn't claim responsibility for the motion. Quickly Ethan stripped off his clothes, then changed into a bathing suit. Before leaving the room, he made sure the desk drawer was closed all the way, the ring hidden once again.

6

Are we not supposed to talk about this or what?
Elli wondered the next day at breakfast. *Am I supposed to pretend I'm oblivious?* Her mother had gone out with Mr. Ransom again the night before; now Mrs. Wells was drinking her coffee and reading the Farm and Garden section of the local newspaper as if this was any other morning.

Well, maybe she's not going to bring it up, but that doesn't mean I can't, Elli decided as she stirred milk into her tea. "So, Mom," she said, forcing herself to smile as though it were all a big joke, "did you have a good time last night?"

Mrs. Wells looked up from the paper. She hesitated for an instant, then smiled back. "Yes, we did."

"Where did you go?" asked Elli.

Her mother put the newspaper aside and folded her arms on top of the table. "Well, let's see. We drove to Spring Valley—stopped in Sherburne on the way so I could pick up a few things at that great yarn store. We had dinner at a new Italian restaurant in Spring Valley and then listened to the concert on the town green. Then we drove back."

"Hmm." Elli loaded the vague syllable with implication. "Sounds like a nice night."

"It was," Mrs. Wells agreed, her smile starting to show the strain.

This is too weird, Elli thought, suddenly wishing that Mrs. Chapman or Ethan were at the table to help her find a way out of this conversation. *It's like our roles have been totally reversed. I'm quizzing Mom about a date, for God's sake.* Her judgment told her to drop the subject—it was just too loaded. But another part of her had to keep pressing. "I thought, though . . ." Elli shifted in her chair and reached for the jar of raspberry jam. "Well, you said you and Mr. Ransom were . . . just friends."

Mrs. Wells flushed slightly and ran a hand through her dark hair. "Well, we are, of course. Good friends."

"Oh, come off it, Mom," Elli burst out. "I heard you come in at two in the morning. The concert at Spring Valley didn't last that long, did it?"

Now the color drained from Mrs. Wells's face and she fixed her daughter with a cool gaze. "My private life isn't your business, honey. I hope you'll try to respect my feelings the way I respect yours."

Elli didn't know how to respond. She dropped her eyes and fiddled with her silverware. After a tense, silent moment, Mrs. Wells pushed back her chair. "Have a nice day sailing," she said as she left the breakfast room.

Have a nice day? You respect my privacy and I'll respect yours? Elli bit back tears of anger and confusion. *Is this how it's going to be, living with a divorced parent? It's like we're not even mother and daughter anymore, just two people stuck sharing the same house.*

She looked up at the sound of footsteps. Her grandmother, dressed in a pink T-shirt and faded chambray overalls, stood in the doorway with an armful of freshly cut flowers. "The garden is the best it's been in years," Mrs. Chapman announced cheerfully. "Plenty of sun and just the right amount of rain. There's nothing like flowers in a house to lift your spirits." Then she frowned, catching sight of Elli's expression. "Dear, is something wrong?"

Elli sighed. "I think I just ticked Mom off. I didn't mean to. Or maybe I did." She shook her head. "I don't know. I just don't know what to think."

Mrs. Chapman took a tall crystal vase from the sideboard and began arranging the flowers. "You mean about your mother and Holling."

Elli nodded. "It seems totally out of the blue,

93

but at the same time it's . . . I mean, he's our *neighbor*. He's lived right next door all these years."

"They've known each other since they were children," Mrs. Chapman confirmed.

"So they've known each other forever, and then all of a sudden they're . . . interested in each other." *Or maybe not all of a sudden,* Elli thought, remembering what she'd seen—or what she thought she'd seen—at the Midsummer Madness ball the previous summer. She studied her grandmother's impassive face. "*Is* it all of a sudden?" she asked point-blank. "Or did something start last summer?"

Mrs. Chapman looked up from her flowers. "I don't know, Eleanor," she replied, her tone formal. "And if I did, I don't think it would be my place to tell you."

"I know, I know," said Elli impatiently. "Mom's private life is none of my business—she told me that herself. But what about the fact that—" She broke off, struggling to put her feelings into words. "I mean, she's my mother. This is my family. It affects me and Ethan. We can't not care about what goes on. And Dad's still . . ." Her voice shook a little. "He's still her husband. Isn't he?"

Mrs. Chapman sighed. "I love you and Ethan, dear. I love your father. And I love Grace. Now that she's an adult, I don't question her actions. I raised her to make her own choices and take responsibility for them. I think it's best to let things evolve, take their course."

"But what if what she's doing is *wrong?*" demanded Elli.

"Is it wrong?" Mrs. Chapman asked. "How can we know? How can we judge?"

Elli shook her head, deeply dissatisfied with this answer. "You can't be so theoretical about it, Nana. It's not about knowing or judging. It's about feeling. And I can't pretend I don't feel bad. I *won't* pretend."

Her grandmother smiled gently. "So it's no use advising you not to fret."

"Nope," said Elli.

"Well, as long as you can be polite," said Mrs. Chapman, placing one last spray of daisies in the vase. "Because your mother might not have mentioned it, but Holling Ransom is joining us for dinner tonight."

Elli's jaw dropped. She stared after her grandmother, who lifted the vase and turned to carry it into the next room. So much for having some time to get used to the idea of her mother dating Mr. Ransom.

"Isn't it just too funny?" said Charlotte with a sly, insinuating smile. "The new boyfriend gets to meet the family. Of course, the new boyfriend happens to be the old next-door neighbor, but still. I really can't wait to witness this moment."

It was late afternoon, and she and Elli were checking that the sailboats were all securely tied to the cleats on the dock. At Charlotte's remark, Elli's face turned pale. "You—*you're* coming over tonight, too?" she stuttered.

Charlotte smiled again, savoring Elli's discomfort. "Your mom invited me," she confirmed, "but I have so much to do tonight, I probably won't make it." *Not that it's not tempting,* Charlotte added to herself. *It's going to be totally awkward and miserable, and I could make it more so.* But dinner with Elli's family didn't fit in with Charlotte's current ploy—to reignite Ethan's interest by playing hard to get. "It *is* funny, though, isn't it?" she pressed, crouching to tighten the line on one of the sailboats. "Making one happy family out of two dysfunctional families. Maybe someday you and I will be sisters, Elli."

At this suggestion, Elli looked literally sick. "Um, well, everything looks okay here," she said in a rush, taking a few giant steps back from Charlotte. "Gotta go—see you later."

Elli rushed off and Charlotte sat back on her heels, laughing to herself. *It's always been too easy to get under Elli's skin,* she mused. Charlotte was as appalled as anybody by the thought of their parents together, permanently or otherwise, but at this point she knew how to keep herself separate, to be an observer. She'd

96

become skilled at pulling the strings behind the scenes rather than acting as one of the puppets onstage. *Dad taught me something,* she thought, a faint taste of bitterness on her tongue.

She stood up and brushed her hands off on her shorts. Clouds had stolen across the sky and the afternoon was chilly. She decided to go for a cup of coffee.

As she approached the clubhouse the door opened and Laura emerged—Laura by herself, without Ethan. *She's pretty, but not gorgeous,* Charlotte observed, taking in Laura's long sandy-brown hair, the dark brown eyes, the classic, even features. *Decent figure, mediocre legs.*

When she saw Charlotte, Laura stopped in her tracks, looking momentarily startled. Then she smiled, her expression guarded but friendly. "Hi, Charlotte."

"Hi, Laura," Charlotte replied in as cheerful a tone as she could manage. "How's it going?"

"Oh, fine. I just finished up some sketches—costumes for the play the kids are putting on for Midsummer Madness weekend."

"You are just so talented," Charlotte told her. "It was pretty lucky for Silver Beach that you decided to spend the summer with Ethan."

Laura let out a slightly uncomfortable laugh. "I don't know about that, but I'm having fun."

"I'm glad." Charlotte smiled, then put a hand

on Laura's arm—a warm, impulsive gesture. "Come back inside and have a cup of coffee with me," she urged. "You know, we've hardly had a chance to talk, just the two of us."

Laura hesitated, glancing over her shoulder as if she hoped someone might come to her rescue. But they were alone. "Well, okay," she agreed. "Yeah, coffee sounds good."

Once they'd bought their coffee at the snack bar, Charlotte steered them toward a corner table by a window overlooking the deck and the cove. She sat down facing Laura, cupping the hot drink in her hands. "So, you like Silver Beach?" she began.

Laura sipped her coffee. "Oh, I love it. It's really idyllic."

"Idyllic." Charlotte smiled. "I don't know about that."

"Maybe it doesn't seem that way if you're here all the time, every summer," Laura amended. "But to an outsider . . ."

"But you're not an outsider," said Charlotte. "You're practically part of the family, aren't you?"

Laura blushed. "I guess so. Yeah, they make me feel that way."

"I'm sure they all just love you to pieces because you make Ethan so happy," Charlotte commented, her tone artfully sincere.

"Umm," said Laura, looking out toward the cove.

"He's really something, isn't he?"

Laura shot a glance at her, veiled and wary. "Ethan?"

Charlotte laughed. "Of *course* Ethan!"

Laura shifted in her seat. "Uh, yeah. He is."

Charlotte leaned forward, her arms folded on the table. "I mean, needless to say, he and I are a thing of the past," she purred, her tone knowing and conspiratorial, "but I have very fond memories of Ethan. *Very* fond."

An uncertain half smile flickered briefly across Laura's face. "Well . . . I'm glad."

"I mean, hey." Charlotte's laughter was low in her throat. "We're big girls, right? We can say it. He's great in the sack, and that's a definite plus when it comes to a relationship, eh?"

A fierce blush crept up Laura's throat to her face. *So modest and embarrassed,* thought Charlotte with a malicious flicker of pleasure. "Oh, come on," she teased Laura. "We can talk about it woman to woman, can't we?"

"I'd rather not— Ethan and I don't—" Laura balled up her napkin and threw it on the table, then looked at her watch. "Oh, wow. It's later than I thought."

Charlotte hadn't missed a single nuance. *They're not sleeping together,* she deduced. *Hmm, very interesting.*

Laura slid her chair back from the table. "Thanks for the coffee. It was . . . talking to you . . ." She waved a distracted good-bye, then disappeared.

Charlotte slumped comfortably in her own seat, her lips curved in a smile. It was just so amusing, making people squirm, making them jump. Puppets on a string.

And Ethan and Laura weren't having sex. *I'll bet he wants to, but she's keeping herself pure,* Charlotte thought disdainfully. Well, it was Laura's loss. And possibly Charlotte's gain. Her eyes narrowed, the blue smoking over with pleasurable speculation. In recent days, she'd felt herself stealing back a portion of Ethan's attention—small, but tangible. And now she had this interesting little tidbit. Yes, it was good to know these things. She was dead certain that sooner or later she'd be able to use it to her advantage. Dead certain.

"I'll have some more of that couscous-and-artichoke-heart salad, if you would," Mr. Ransom requested, smiling across the table at Elli. She passed the dish and he spooned another helping onto his plate. "Did you say you made this, Elli? What's the secret ingredient?"

Elli shrugged. "Nothing, really. Just some fresh herbs from the garden. Dill, mint. And walnuts—toasted walnuts."

"Ah. That's where the crunch comes from. Well, it's delicious."

"Uh, thanks." She glanced at her brother to

see if he too thought it was strange to be sitting at the dinner table talking to Mr. Ransom about couscous-and-artichoke-heart salad. Ethan was pushing the food around on his plate with his fork, not really eating.

Mrs. Wells more than compensated for her children's lack of enthusiasm. "Try the new potatoes," she urged Mr. Ransom, beaming. "They're from the garden, too." *She looks like a lovesick teenager,* Elli reflected, losing what little appetite she'd had.

Mrs. Chapman was eating quietly, her alert eyes taking in every detail of the scene, the nuances of each exchange. Meanwhile, Laura was clearly making an effort to take up the slack for Elli and Ethan. "I loved your last novel, Mr. Ransom. We have them all at home—my parents are big fans, too. When will the next one come out?"

"Perhaps as early as next summer," he replied. "I'm on the third draft, but it still needs further revision. Shaping." His smile was wry, charming. "It's quite a long and tedious process, really. Not nearly as glamorous as nonwriters imagine."

Laura looked fascinated. "It must be inspiring, living someplace as beautiful as Silver Beach."

Mr. Ransom glanced meaningfully at Mrs. Wells. "Yes, it is. Silver Beach has always been a source for me. A deep, rich vein that I'll probably spend the rest of my life mining."

Mrs. Wells shot Laura a sly glance. "If you'd known him as a kid, you'd never have guessed that he'd turn into someone so *distinguished*. He was a real Dennis the Menace, the king of practical jokes."

"I grew out of it," Mr. Ransom protested good-naturedly.

"Yeah, by the time you were in college. Then you were more into the moody James Dean mode," she teased.

"So you're saying I never created an original character in my life," he said with mock despair. "Lord, don't tell my publisher!"

Elli tore off a piece of French bread, then abandoned it on her plate. She couldn't wait for the meal to end. Normally she enjoyed Mr. Ransom's company—though he had a reputation in the colony for being cold and reclusive, he'd always treated her kindly. But since he'd started seeing her mother, she really didn't know how to act around him. And she knew her brother, who'd taken his cues from Charlotte's unhappiness with her home life, had never liked him. *Here he is, sitting in Grandpa's chair like he's a part of the family, and we're just supposed to adjust?* thought Elli.

When her mother started to clear the table, Elli jumped up to help. "We'll bring in the coffee and dessert," Mrs. Wells told the others. "The rest of you stay put."

In the kitchen, Elli arranged cookies on a plate while her mother squeezed fresh lime juice over the fruit salad. "It's going well, don't you think?" Mrs. Wells asked cheerfully.

Elli stared at her mother. Could she really be that self-centered, that dense? Had she completely forgotten their conversation that morning at breakfast? "What do you mean, going well?" Elli burst out. "What's this dumb dinner supposed to accomplish?"

Mrs. Wells stiffened at Elli's tone. "I'd appreciate your being civil when we have company," she said coolly.

"I've been plenty civil," Elli retorted. "And Mr. Ransom isn't 'company.' This isn't some cozy neighborhood potluck. He's your . . . your *lover*." She spat out the word, embarrassed just by the sound of it.

Her mother fixed her with a stern glare. "You're out of line, young lady."

"No, *you're* out of line," Elli cried, hurling the last few cookies down on the plate. "You cheated last summer, didn't you? And you're cheating now. That's what it is, because you're still married to Dad. Maybe you don't live with him, but you live with us, and you're not acting like our mother."

Whirling, she ran for the door, blinded by angry tears.

"Elli, come back here this—" The door

slammed behind her, cutting off her mother's words like a blade. Elli kept running across the dark lawn, through the dune grass that slashed at her bare legs, and out onto the sand.

She sucked in deep breaths of misty night air, struggling to sort out her confused thoughts. Then, blinking back tears, she focused on a figure standing at the water's edge, a familiar figure, someone she knew and loved. Yes, loved.

She hurried toward him, her eyes shining now with hope. Sam had come to find her, just as he had almost every night the summer before, when they'd meet in the moonlight, just the two of them, to talk and swim. He'd come for her—he'd known somehow that she needed him, that it was time to forget the past, to start over. "Sam," she whispered.

A current vibrated through the air, hot and electric, drawing them closer. Sam stepped toward her, one arm lifted as if to touch her. "Elli, what . . . ?"

Then Elli glimpsed a movement out of the corner of her eye. Someone else was approaching from the south end of the beach. A slim, curvy girl with shiny auburn hair.

Of course—Sam had a rendezvous with Julia. His girlfriend. *He's not here to see me after all.* Elli recoiled in mortification. *Oh, God, just get out of here before you make an even bigger fool of yourself.*

Sam's fingertips brushed Elli's arm as she turned away. Did he whisper, "Wait, don't go"? No, it was only her pathetic imagination playing tricks on her. She quickened her pace, refusing to look back over her shoulder, to witness the kiss of greeting between Sam and Julia. She was nearly running, though she didn't know where. There was no place to go, no one to turn to. She wished she could run away from Silver Beach altogether, leave it all behind.

7

When Elli spotted Sam on her way to the dock the next morning, she almost did a one-eighty and bolted in the opposite direction. *Act your age,* she lectured herself silently. He was right smack in between her and her destination—there was no way to avoid him. *Just say hi and breeze on by.*

"Morning," she said cheerfully, not quite meeting his eyes.

"Morning," Sam echoed.

She was almost in the clear when he spoke again. "El . . . are you all right? I mean, last night I got the impression you were . . . well, upset about something."

She turned to face him. "Oh, sorry about that," she said, keeping her tone casual. "I looked like a wreck, huh? Yeah, I had a fight with my mom. No big deal. We made up. Sort of."

106

"Well," he said, looking at her with sympathetic eyes, "just so long as you know that if you ever need someone to talk to . . ."

Elli felt herself hardening. *So now he thinks I'm a total charity case,* she thought. "Thanks, but I know you're really busy. Training for the regatta with Julia," she added pointedly.

"Right, the regatta. Yeah, it takes up a lot of time." He smiled. "Not that it's a chore being on the water all day. You know, if you want to go out on the *Dollar* sometime, the offer still stands."

For a moment they just stood looking at each other, Sam waiting for Elli's answer, Elli wishing she could say what her heart really wanted her to say: *Yes.*

Her momentary annoyance had passed, replaced by all the other emotions Sam stirred up inside her. As she looked into his warm hazel eyes a longing pierced her, sharp as a knife. *We'd sail for hours, the wind and spray in our faces, and then drop anchor off Blueberry Island and swim to shore. Lie in the sun, talk.* She pushed the image from her mind—she smothered the memory of Sam's strong arms around her the year before, the night of the Midsummer Madness ball. It was impossible, out of reach, a stupid fantasy. "Sometime," Elli repeated vaguely. "See ya."

"See ya."

Sam walked off toward the water. When Elli turned on her heel, heading for the soda machine in the clubhouse, she found that Laura had come up behind her.

"Well, that settles it," said Laura as she and Elli walked together to the soda machine.

"What settles what?" asked Elli, pushing open the door to the clubhouse.

Laura lowered her voice. "You and Sam DeWitt are madly in love with each other."

Elli dropped her change on the floor. "Yeah, right," she snorted, bending to scoop up the quarters and dimes. "Laura, where do you *get* these ideas?"

"By keeping my eyes open. It's written all over both your faces."

"Sam's dating someone else," Elli reminded Laura, popping quarters into the machine. "And we were never really— I mean, it didn't go beyond— And that was last summer, anyway. *Ages* ago."

"It's still there, though," Laura argued with a knowing smile. "The chemistry. The attraction. Admit it."

Elli punched a button and a can of soda rolled out of the machine with a thunk. "What do you want?" she asked Laura.

"Diet."

Another punch, another thunk. Cold cans in hand, they walked back outside. Elli popped the top on her soda, took a long sip, then looked at

Laura. "You really have a way of cutting right to the core. Man, am I that transparent?"

"No," Laura assured her. "But what I don't understand is, if you two love each other and always have, what are you *doing?*"

"Going nuts," said Elli with a rueful laugh. "I am, anyway." It was an incredible relief to finally say it aloud. "I am so completely jealous of Julia I could scream! And when Sam asked her instead of me to sail in the regatta with him, it just about—" *Broke my heart.* She looked down, unable to say the words.

"I know," Laura said softly. "I bet it hurt. And I can't say I understand his motives. But I'll tell you one thing: Maybe they're still training together for the regatta, but Sam and Julia are definitely cooling off in the romance department."

Elli cocked an eyebrow. "They sure still look like a couple." She recalled the tryst on the beach the night before. "And act like a couple."

"Maybe," said Laura, "but I have it straight from Sam."

Elli's curiosity was piqued. "He actually said something?"

Laura nodded. "You know, when he was giving me some water-skiing tips yesterday? Well, out of the blue, he's telling me that he's not that serious about Julia. The relationship is nothing special, they just hang out together for lack of anything better to do. I mean, it didn't have *any-*

thing to do with what we were talking about, but he made this *point*. Hoping, I'm sure, that I'd pass it along to you," she concluded.

For a moment Elli's spirits soared. Then, quickly, she brought herself back down to earth. "I don't know," she said cautiously. "I mean, if he's not into it, if he'd rather ask out . . . someone else . . . why doesn't he just do it?"

"Why are *you* dating Chad?" Laura countered.

Elli looked at the ground.

"Obviously not everyone dates the person they're really into," Laura said gently. "So stop being so prickly and defensive and just go after him. He'll meet you halfway—I guarantee it."

Elli wished it were that simple. The fact was, Sam was dating Julia and Elli was dating Chad. *And Chad really likes me,* she added to herself. Even if what Laura said was true, how could she and Sam ever untangle the webs they'd woven and find their way back to each other?

Late in the day, Ethan and Laura sat on the porch rockers, munching chips and salsa and watching the sunset. The rumbling sound of a motorcycle broke the peaceful interlude.

Ethan looked toward the Briarwood driveway, shading his eyes against the last rays of light, as the Harley came to a stop. Charlotte was sitting behind some shaggy-haired guy in black leather, her arms wrapped around his waist.

110

Ethan shifted his gaze back to the sunset.

"Who's that guy?" Laura asked conversationally.

Ethan shrugged. "Some local. Don't know him personally, but I know *of* him. Not the most clean-cut character in the Glen. A druggie."

"Hmm," murmured Laura.

Ethan reached for a tortilla chip. The guy had killed the engine on his bike, and now snatches of conversation drifted across the dusky lawn. "Maybe I don't feel like it," Charlotte said, her voice high-pitched and quarrelsome.

"Maybe it doesn't matter what you feel like," the guy replied in a threatening tone.

Ethan couldn't resist looking again. Laura too was transfixed. The guy stepped toward Charlotte, one hand lifted.

As Ethan lurched forward in the rocker, ready to sprint across the lawn, he felt Laura grip his arm. "Ethan, cool it," she said. "You don't need to go to her rescue. It's not your business anymore."

"But I can't help it . . . it's almost Midsummer Madness, and I know she gets crazy this time of year."

"Look, she's *fine*," Laura insisted. "Listen to them."

Laura was right—the spat was over. Now Charlotte and the guy were laughing; he leaned back against the wall of the garage and she pressed her body to his. Even from a distance, it was obvious that the kiss was long and hard, not just lips touching but full body contact right down to the toes.

Ethan let out his breath. "You're right. It's not my business anymore."

"Let's go inside," said Laura, rising to her feet.

They left the chips and salsa and went upstairs. In his room, Ethan pulled the shade to block out the view of Briarwood. Laura sat on the edge of his bed, skimming a dog-eared sports magazine.

He joined her, took the magazine from her hands, and then looked into her eyes, stroking her hair. "So . . . we have about an hour until dinner," he said with a smile. "How about a nap?" Laura laughed and they lay back on the bed, their arms wrapped around each other. Ethan rubbed her back until he felt the tension drain from her body. "It's warm in here," he observed.

"Maybe it's you."

Sitting up, Ethan stripped off his T-shirt. He looked down at Laura, tracing the line of her throat with his fingertip. "You're warm, too," he said, sliding his hand to her shoulder. "Maybe you should lose some of these clothes."

She eased out of her shirt and then, after a moment's hesitation, unzipped her shorts. They lay back down, both wearing just their underwear. Ethan moved his hands lightly over her body. Her suntanned skin was warm, smooth, soft. Laura nuzzled her face against his neck, and then her lips found his.

It took only a moment for the kiss to become intensely passionate. Ethan unhooked Laura's bra, and then his hands moved down her hips to the elastic of her bikini underpants. "Hey, quit it," she said, playful and breathless. When he didn't, she rolled away from him. "Ethan, I said stop."

Breathing deep and fast, Ethan lifted his hands, cupping her face. "I wasn't going to— I only want to look at you," he promised. "You're so beautiful. I swear I won't—"

She shook her head vehemently. "We've talked about this before. You know we have to draw the line somewhere. It feels too good. We'd get carried away, and . . . I'm just not ready."

"But I love you. And you love me," he reasoned.

"That doesn't automatically mean we should." She bit her lip, averting her eyes. "I know you did it with— I know you *probably* did it with Charlotte. And I'm sorry if I don't . . . satisfy you."

"Hey, don't talk like that," Ethan said.

"It's true, though, isn't it?" She lifted her eyes again, fixing him with an earnest, searching gaze. "You feel as though something's missing. I can tell."

He shook his head, suddenly ashamed of himself, though he wasn't sure why. "Nothing's missing. You're perfect. And if you want to wait, I'll wait. It'll be worth it." He cracked a smile, trying to lighten the mood. "We don't have to hold out till we're *married*, though, do we?"

Laura's expression remained serious. "I don't know. I don't know when it will feel right to me, when I'll feel mature enough to handle it. Can you accept that?"

"Give me some credit." Ethan dropped a kiss on her forehead. "I'm not a sex maniac. And like I said, I love you." He grinned again. "With and without your clothes on."

This time she did smile. "Thanks."

The passion had cooled and now they lay quietly, Laura's head on Ethan's shoulder. Soon he felt her relax into sleep, but he stayed awake, staring at the ceiling. It couldn't hurt to *think* about making love with Laura, so he tried to imagine what it would be like. He couldn't. Instead, another picture filled his brain, infused his body with a memory of ultimate desire, ultimate fulfillment. *Laura's the one I want to be with,* he told himself, but that didn't stop the pictures from coming, from taking over. Memories of making love . . . with Charlotte.

"Midsummer Madness," said Laura, her forehead crinkled. "Why do they call it that?"

She and Elli were in the kitchen, doing the dishes after dinner. "You know, I never really thought about it until last summer, and then Nana told me," Elli replied, turning on the

114

faucet. "First, there's the weather. There were lots of summer storms and shipwrecks on the Great Lakes in the old days. But basically she said it was because everyone onshore gets a little crazy in the August heat. They fight more, fall in love more, as if all emotions get taken to the extreme. So the colony invented this holiday—lots of games and competitions, ice cream and watermelon—to tire people out and cool them off."

Laura laughed. "And does it work?"

Elli gave her a funny look. "It's hard to say."

They worked in silence for a few minutes, Elli rinsing plates and glasses, Laura loading them into the dishwasher. Half a dozen times, Laura shot a glance at Elli, getting ready to speak. *I believe in Midsummer Madness,* she wanted to say. *It's happening. It's happening to Ethan and me. Something's happening, anyway. Something's coming unglued.*

But Elli wasn't just her friend. First and foremost, she was Ethan's sister. The two girls had grown close over the course of the summer, but there was one thing they didn't really talk about, and that was Laura's relationship with Ethan. Laura knew Elli approved and assumed everything was great. *And it was, when we got to Silver Beach,* Laura recalled. *But now?*

She thought about the scene before dinner, seeing Charlotte with that awful guy, and then upstairs in Ethan's bedroom. What was it about Charlotte? Laura hadn't been able to tear her own eyes away from her; she couldn't stop thinking about her. And if Laura responded so strongly, what did Ethan feel?

Laura bent to put a plate in the dishwasher, hiding her expression behind a curtain of hair. On the surface, Ethan was more attentive to her than ever, but there were times when she felt that he was drifting away from her—even during their most intimate moments, even when he was holding her in his arms. *I don't know what's on his mind anymore,* Laura thought, *what he's thinking.*

She couldn't help it—tears welled in her eyes, and one rolled down her cheek. Sniffling, she brought the dishtowel to her face.

"Laura, what's wrong?" Elli asked, startled and concerned.

"Oh, nothing," said Laura, managing a smile, though her eyes were still bright with unshed tears. "I was just thinking, and all of a sudden I felt really . . . homesick."

Elli slipped an arm around Laura's waist and gave her a supportive squeeze. "I know. We're so glad to have you with us, we keep forgetting that we're not your family. You should invite your folks up here for a weekend. Or take the car and go home for a few days."

"Oh, I'll be all right," Laura assured her. She

116

crossed the kitchen and took a tissue from a box on the window sill. "This has been the best summer of my life. Really. I don't want to miss a minute of Silver Beach. And if I left now, even for a few days . . . I'd miss all the fun: Midsummer Madness weekend, the play the kids are performing, your tennis tournament, the regatta, the costume ball."

"It *will* be fun," Elli promised her. "We'll make sure you have a good time. You won't miss Winnetka for a second."

At dawn, Charlotte dismounted from the back of the Harley, the heels of her boots scuffing the gravel. Nick flashed her a sexy grin, then gunned the motor. *Waking up half the residents of the colony, no doubt,* Charlotte thought with a smirk as she tramped toward the house. *And they'll know who to blame. Holling Ransom's motherless, out-of-control daughter. Out all night. Again. Scandalous!*

She went inside, not caring that the screen door slammed loudly behind her. Let it wake her dad up—maybe he'd wonder where she'd been, whom she'd been with. Maybe he'd worry, get mad, lecture her, ground her. Yeah, right.

She paused before climbing the stairs. The house was so quiet. All around her, she could feel the presence of things . . . furniture, carpets, drapes. Lifeless things, dead things. Somewhere

117

upstairs, her father slept, but she couldn't feel his presence. They lived in a museum, frozen in time, as cold, separate, and insensitive as figures of wax. Turning away from the staircase, Charlotte retraced her steps. The door to her father's study was closed but unlocked.

She entered, shivering. Of all the rooms in the big house, this was the coldest. *The coldest because it's the most Dad,* she thought, her eyes roving over the bookshelves, the writing table with computer and typewriter, the piles of manuscripts. His room, his space; his strong, authorly thoughts flavored the air even when he wasn't present.

With a start, Charlotte realized that it had been a solid year since she'd last set foot in the study. On the rare occasions when she had a reason to communicate with him, she stopped at the door, knocked, and called in to him. He never invited her in. No one went in, not even the maid. *Did Mom?* Charlotte wondered, glancing at Annette Ransom's photograph on the desk. Was that photograph the only part of her ever allowed into the sanctuary?

Elli was invited in, though, Charlotte thought as she retreated to the hall and went upstairs for a shower. Mr. Ransom had let Elli look at his collection of autographed first editions, and the previous summer Elli had given him some dumb software program for writers—he'd loved that. And now maybe he invited Grace Wells.

Charlotte stepped into the shower and turned on the water, as hot as she could stand it. As the scalding drops pelted her bare skin, she tried to make herself cry. *Midsummer Madness is this weekend. Two more days and it's nine years since Mom walked into the lake,* she thought. *I can't even remember her birthday anymore, just the day she died.* But the tears wouldn't come. Hot water streamed down Charlotte's body, but her eyes remained dry. There was no soothing the ache in her heart, the hunger in her soul.

"This trunk here," said Mrs. Chapman, fumbling with the latch. "Open it, will you, Elli? These old hinges are awfully stiff."

It was the Friday before Midsummer Madness weekend and Elli and Laura were searching for ball dresses in the attic. Elli hauled up the lid of the leatherbound trunk, and Laura reached in for a sleeveless, champagne-pink dress stitched all over with glittering silver beads.

"I'm so glad the theme of this year's ball is the Jazz Age," Laura said excitedly. "I've always wanted to dress like a flapper."

"This'll be a blast," Elli agreed, choosing a pale gold sheath. For a moment she imagined herself in the dress, moving across the dance floor in Sam's arms—and then banished the image. Despite what Laura had told her about

Sam's hints, Elli couldn't let herself get her hopes up. "Last year it was the Edwardian period—pinched waists, floor-length skirts, button-up shoes. Dull."

"So what do you think?" asked Laura, holding the pink dress against her body. She twirled so both Elli and Mrs. Chapman could admire her.

"You'll look just like Daisy in *The Great Gatsby*," said Elli.

Her grandmother tipped her head to one side. "No, you'll look just like Eliza Chapman."

"Eliza Chapman?" Laura repeated. "Who's that?"

"Eliza was Horace's aunt," Mrs. Chapman explained. "Oh, she was a wild thing. I remember the night she wore that dress." She nodded, a pensive expression on her face. "It was this very weekend, Midsummer Madness, years before Horace and I began seeing each other. Eliza's best friend, Roxanne Ransom, wore the exact same dress—they had them made to match at a chic dressmaker's in Chicago. Those two did everything together, and they were *bad*. Yes, I can just picture them on the deck of the yacht club, long cigarette holders in their fingers, drinking bootleg liquor right along with the men. I was just a girl—how I admired their spunk!"

"What will you wear to the ball, Nana?" asked Elli.

Mrs. Chapman sighed. "To tell you the truth, I

don't believe I'll go this year. Just don't have the heart for it."

Now that Grandpa's gone, Elli thought sadly. "Are you sure?" she asked gently. "It won't be the same without you."

"Thanks, dear, but I'm sure," Mrs. Chapman replied. She smiled at Laura. "I have a stack of library books on my night table and if I don't read them soon, the Silver Glen library is going to fine me but good."

"Help us pick out some accessories, then," Elli urged. "There must be jewelry somewhere, those long swingy necklaces and feather boas and stuff."

"Actually, if you don't mind, I think I'll leave you two to it. I'm a bit tired," said Mrs. Chapman, starting down the steep, narrow stairs. "Look in the bottom of the trunk. I'm sure you'll find plenty of silly things."

They did find jewelry and feather boas and funny little beaded caps. Laura modeled them all, laughing, but Elli couldn't quite get into the spirit. "It's so different from last year," she said finally. "Poor Nana. Things are so different now, with Grandpa gone."

Laura nodded sympathetically. "It must be really tough on you all."

Elli forced herself to smile. "But at least you're here." She decided not to tell Laura all the other reasons that Midsummer Madness seemed an ominous, depressing time to her. *The an-niversary of Charlotte's mother's death. Last summer, Mom and Mr. Ransom, and Mom and Dad's big blowup, and Charlotte cheating on Ethan with Sloan. And Sam's and my first and last kiss.* Once again, Elli pushed the memories from her mind. "It's fun having someone new to share this with. I'm really getting psyched."

"I can't wait for everybody to see the play the kids have been working on," said Laura. "It's truly hilarious. Oh, that reminds me—I have to meet Ethan at the clubhouse to put a few finishing touches on the sets. I should probably get going. See you later, okay?"

"Bye, Laura."

Laura made her way down the stairs, the pink dress and a couple of necklaces draped over her arm. Elli still hadn't decided on accessories, but with both her grandmother and Laura gone, the attic suddenly felt oppressively quiet, musty, and warm. Taking the whole box of jewelry as well as the gold beaded dress, Elli too returned to the second floor.

In her own room, she hung the dress carefully in her closet. Then she sat cross-legged on her bed and dumped the jewelry box upside down. Necklaces, bracelets, and earrings cascaded onto the bedspread with a pleasant jingle. But just before Elli began sorting through them, she noticed the box itself. *Looks like it has a se-*

cret compartment in the bottom! she thought, noting the tiny brass hinge. *Maybe there are some real gems hidden inside.*

Holding the box upside down on her knee, Elli used her fingernail to pry open the bottom. She held her breath, expecting to see the flash and glitter of diamonds. Instead all the compartment contained was a slender packet of letters. *Maybe Eliza wrote them,* she speculated to herself. But something about the letters looked relatively modern—they were bundled together with a rubber band, and the paper was still white rather than yellowed with age.

Curious, Elli removed the packet and slipped off the rubber band. There were ten letters in all. "Notes, really," she observed, opening one. "Just a few lines." Then she saw the name scrawled at the top of the page and her heart skipped a beat. The first note was dated nine years earlier and began, *Dearest Grace . . .*

Elli knew she should put the letters back; they belonged to her mother, they were personal. And Grace had hidden them away—obviously she didn't intend anyone to see them. *She hid them,* Elli thought. *From Dad?*

She knew she shouldn't keep reading, but she couldn't stop herself. *Dearest Grace, One more hour—promise you'll be there. I can't get through the day without a taste of you. Don't make me wait like last night; just come. I know it's insane, but I almost don't care if we get caught. H.*

Rapidly, Elli read the second note and then the third, the pages dropping one after another onto the bed. They were all similar in tone and style: brief but wildly passionate, at times almost poetic. All were dated from the first part of the summer nine years earlier; all were addressed to Grace, all signed only with the initial *H.*

As the last note slipped from her fingers, Elli sank back against the pillows, stunned. *Mom had an affair,* she thought, her head spinning. She was married, she had little kids—but she'd been seeing someone on the sly. Someone right there in Silver Beach! And there was only one person it could be, Elli knew, only one man who could write such sensuous prose. Only one H.

8

"We're in the finals, Elli!" Chad cheered as they walked off the court. They had just beaten Heather and Hugh in the semifinals of the Midsummer Madness junior tennis tournament.

Mechanically Elli returned Chad's hug. "Thanks to you and all your aces."

"It wasn't just me," he protested. "You were great. You didn't miss a shot, I swear. I've never seen anyone cover the court so well."

Elli couldn't remember a single shot she'd made. She could think of nothing but the love letters to her mother from H. Her body had been on its own. *Maybe that's why I played well,* Elli thought distractedly. *I was like a robot, preprogrammed, just reacting. No chance to psych myself out.* "Who do we play in the finals?" she asked.

"Amber and Doug. We've beaten them before." His arm tightened around her waist.

"We're gonna win, El," he exulted. "I can feel it. Can't you?"

"Yeah," she said, unable to echo his emotion.

A short while later, they stood across the net from Doug and Amber. Amber served first, to Elli, who sliced a deep backhand to Doug. Chad was poised at the net to volley the shot. They won the point.

Match point was a long, heart-stopping rally, and when Doug hit the ball into the net, the crowd of spectators leaped to their feet, clapping and whistling. Again, Chad and Elli had triumphed with relative ease.

Chad and Elli trotted forward to shake their friends' hands and then Chad grasped Elli around the waist and swung her high in the air. When he set her down, he planted a kiss on her lips.

Elli laughed, waving to Ethan and Laura, who'd been watching. Then Elli waved at her mother, who was there with Mr. Ransom, but her smile was stiff.

Mrs. Fairleigh came up with the small silver bowl traditionally presented to the tournament victors. "Congratulations on a fine match," she said, beaming. "Elli, you certainly are versatile. Didn't you win the regatta last year?"

Chad playfully ruffled Elli's hair. "She's a star, isn't she?"

Keep smiling, Elli ordered herself. *No reason to bum everyone else out, too.* After all, Chad and

Mrs. Fairleigh couldn't know how much it hurt to be reminded of the past summer's regatta—they couldn't know that this victory paled in comparison. *Tennis just isn't the same,* Elli thought as she held the cold silver bowl in her hands. Tennis was about boundaries: the lines of the court, the net. Sailing was about water, sky, speed, freedom. But it wasn't just the contrast between the two sports, Elli knew. The regatta victory had been thrilling in and of itself, but the most exciting element had been her partnership with Sam. The victory was something they'd worked for together all summer, a dream they'd shared and seen to fruition. True, she and Chad had been practicing for weeks, but it had never reached the same pitch. *And the chemistry between us—is there any?* Elli wondered, suddenly bone tired.

Ethan and Laura pressed their way through the crush to join Elli and Chad. "That was great, you guys," said Laura.

"Best tennis I've seen in Silver Beach all summer," Ethan declared. "How about cooling off with a boat ride? If we head out now, we can catch the end of the regatta."

"I'm kind of wiped out," Elli said quickly when she saw Chad start to nod. She wouldn't be able to stand watching Sam and Julia flying to the finish line on the *Silver Dollar.* "I think I'll just head back to the house and take a shower. See you later, okay?"

As she turned away Chad gently clutched her arm. "Elli," he said softly, his eyes glowing, "thanks for being my partner in the tournament. That was the best part, even better than winning."

"I had a lot of fun."

"I can't wait until tonight." He slid his hand up her arm. "The costume ball."

"Tonight," Elli agreed, with as much warmth as she could muster.

The DeWitts' *Silver Dollar* and the Maddens' *Rampage* were nearly neck and neck as they raced south from Bleakman's Bay. Julia scrambled across the deck of the *Dollar*, adjusting the jib lines; Sam stood firm at the helm. But *Rampage* edged ahead of them.

"Give it all you've got!" Sam shouted to Julia over the roar of the wind as they neared Blueberry Island and the finish line. "We can still catch them!"

The yacht heeled sharply, carving a swift path through the whitecaps of Lake Michigan. They gained a foot on *Rampage*, and then another. But the finish line, marked by a flotilla of small craft with fluttering flags, was coming up fast. Too fast. In the final moments, Sam and Julia and the *Silver Dollar* were edged out.

They let up on the lines, allowing the sails to luff. "So close, but that was still wonderful," Julia exclaimed, with a tired, happy smile.

"The Maddens are tough competition," Sam agreed, ruffling her hair. "You did good."

The smaller boats, loaded with spectators, circled around *Rampage* and started tooting their horns. Sam hollered his congratulations to Forrest Madden and his father and then reefed the sail and started the motor, steering the *Dollar* into the channel to the south of Blueberry Island.

Julia was chattering excitedly about the race. "You know, we lost a little time going around the buoy at Deep River. Maybe if I'd been a little quicker at the helm that time . . . What do you think?"

"I don't think it made a whole lot of difference. You did fine."

"Well, that tack up to Bleakman's Bay—we were practically wallowing there for a few minutes."

"It's not the windiest day," Sam pointed out. "Everybody slowed down in that stretch."

Julia contemplated him, her gray eyes suddenly serious. "You know, you're so competitive, especially when it comes to sailing. How come you're not more disappointed about this?"

Sam shrugged. "Like you said, we should feel good. Second place is nothing to sneeze at."

"Yeah, but last year you came in first—you edged out the Maddens specifically, in fact," Julia reminded him, "and now you have to see the trophy go to someone else."

Sam pictured the ornate, antique silver cup that bore the names of the winners throughout the whole history of the Midsummer Madness regatta. His name was already engraved there, alongside Elli's. *And I'm glad,* he realized, *that it'll stay that way. That my name won't be there with Julia's.*

He shot a guilty glance at her, hoping she couldn't read his mind. She was still gazing somberly at him. "This year was different, wasn't it?" she said. "The race . . . it didn't mean as much to you."

"It meant a lot."

"But not as much."

Sam heaved a sigh. He couldn't lie to her. His heart hadn't been in it this year, not the way it had been the previous summer when he raced with Elli. And heart was what separated winners from losers. "Not as much," Sam admitted finally.

"You still care for her, don't you?" Julia said quietly.

Sam felt another pang of guilt. Suddenly they weren't just talking about the regatta—they were talking about the whole summer, their relationship. He killed the engine and the boat slowed, bobbing in the water. "I care about *you,* Jules," he insisted, taking her hand. "You're incredibly special to me."

"You're special to me, too." She squeezed his hand. "We've had a good time. But Sam, you can't pretend that it's the same as it was the first time we went out, two summers ago. Something happened in between. *Someone* happened."

Again, he couldn't deny it. For a long minute they looked at each other in silence. "So what do we do now?" he asked gruffly.

Julia looked at her hands. "Maybe we should just—just be friends."

"Oh, Jules." Sam wrapped his arms around her, holding her close. "I'm sorry, I really am."

"Me too." She sniffled. "But it's the best thing to do. Better than nothing."

He rubbed her back. "We've always been good friends. That'll never change, I promise."

They held each other for a moment, then drew apart. "You know, it's funny," said Julia. "I'm not really hurt, or mad—just a little sad. I mean, this isn't a total surprise. I've sensed for a while that the feeling was starting to fade." She smiled through the tears. "Sometimes you just come in second, right?"

"You didn't come in second. It's not like that. This other . . . thing, with Elli . . ." Sam looked away from Julia, across the cove, his eyes narrowed. "I still haven't figured it out. I haven't figured *her* out."

Julia laughed. "Why should that stop you? Do you know *anyone* who's figured out love?"

Sam grinned. "Good point."

Julia started the motor and the yacht resumed chugging through the channel. "I don't really feel like talking about this anymore," she

131

said, "but I'll give you one piece of advice: If you're going to go for it, go for it. It's like the race today. You won't win if you don't want it more than anything."

Sam nodded. *And I do want it,* he realized, his heart pounding harder than it had all day, even at the tensest, most exciting moment of the regatta. *I want her.*

Late Saturday afternoon, Charlotte pushed her way through a bank of lilac bushes and walked across the broad green lawn separating Briarwood from the Chapman cottage. The air was heavy and humid with midsummer, and the colony was quiet; everyone was gathered at the clubhouse watching the play that Ethan and Laura's day campers were staging. *Everyone but Dad, who's working, as always—and, as always, couldn't care less that this is the anniversary of Mom's death,* thought Charlotte.

She climbed the steps of the Chapman cottage and crossed the porch. Without knocking, she pushed open the door and stepped into the front hall. For a moment she stood still, listening. *The old lady might have skipped the festivities,* she thought, her ears peeled for the sound of a radio or TV, the gurgle of water running, the creak of a footstep on old floorboards. But there was nothing. She relaxed. The house was empty, as she'd expected.

Charlotte drifted noiselessly upstairs to the second floor. The first bedroom on the hall was Ethan's. The door was ajar; she slipped inside. The room was just as she remembered. She stood by the dresser and touched his belongings, one by one: a magazine, the portable Discman, a plastic comb, a bottle of aftershave. She looked in the closet, and finally sat on the edge of his bed, stroking the rumpled sheets. *Does Laura sneak in at night?* Charlotte wondered. *Do they lie here together?* She reclined full length on the bed, her hands behind her head, smelling Ethan's scent on the pillow. *What do they do together, if they don't have sex?*

The next room was a guest room, but clearly someone was living in it for the summer. Someone—Laura. Charlotte prowled into the room. She opened the dresser drawers, fingering Laura's clothing, examining her jewelry and makeup. There was a stack of paperback books on the dresser, a bouquet of wildflowers in a glass jar, a box of monogrammed stationery. And on the neatly made bed was a pale pink beaded gown.

"That dress!" Charlotte exclaimed out loud. It was exactly like the one she'd found in the attic at Briarwood. Her lips curved in a smile as the delicious possibilities flickered through her mind. *We'll both be pretty in pink. Maybe the ball will be more fun than I thought.*

Finally Charlotte entered Elli's room, next door to Laura's. *Sweet and clean—just what you'd expect,* Charlotte thought. But as she looked around she was surprised at how mixed and elusive her emotions were. *Eleanor Chapman Wells, I've hated you for years,* she mused. *Hated you and envied you.* But that summer, as sailing co-instructors, they'd almost had fun.

She lifted the lid of the cedar blanket chest, bending down to touch the pile of old dolls that lay flung about inside, their soft, faded bodies twisted in various macabre positions. She smiled, recalling the games she and Elli had played as children. Elli had wanted the dolls to cook and clean, play tennis and dress up for parties; Charlotte had wanted them to fight duels, climb trees, be in shipwrecks. "I remember you," Charlotte said to one doll, an antique baby doll with a pink-cheeked porcelain face and a mop of golden curls. "I wanted to shave your head—you were going to join the army. But Elli saved you, eh?"

As she picked up the doll she saw something underneath. Papers of some sort, bound together with a rubber band.

Carrying the papers over to the bed, Charlotte snapped off the rubber band and opened the first note. As she sat, immobile, reading page after page, she had a flash of intuition. *Elli put the notes in the chest. Recently. She found them—she's read them, too. She sat right here and made this very same discovery.*

Charlotte didn't realize she was crying until the hot tears started to splash onto her uplifted hands, onto the notes themselves. She flung the papers aside, overcome by revulsion. "It didn't just start, this affair between Dad and Mrs. Wells," she whispered to the tumbled pile of silent, lifeless dolls. "It was going on nine years ago. When Mom was still alive. That very summer, right before she died."

The implications stabbed straight to her heart, and she hugged herself, rocking with silent sobs. She had known her mother was desperately unhappy, but she had never known precisely why. Now it was crystal clear, as plain as the writing—her father's writing—on the pages in front of her. "I should have guessed," Charlotte choked out, struggling to regain her self-control. Of course there could have been only one reason her mother would have chosen death over life, would have abandoned her eight-year-old daughter, her beloved only child. At last Charlotte had found the key that unlocked the terrible mysteries of the past.

Her tears were drying, but her body continued to shake convulsively. The past wouldn't stay buried. It reached forward with strangling fingers and cold, poisonous breath into the present—and perhaps into the future as well.

Elli crossed the porch of the cottage at dusk, still smiling over the children's play, which had been a comic history of the founding of Silver Beach. Her mother, grandmother, Ethan, and Laura were still at the clubhouse, and Elli was looking forward to some time to herself.

Entering the cottage, Elli gasped. Someone was standing in the dim hallway.

The figure stepped forward out of the shadows. "Oh, Charlotte, it's you." Elli put a hand to her heart. "You scared me half to—" She broke off and frowned. "What are you doing here?"

Charlotte gestured with something in her hand. "Oh, there was a book your grandmother said I could borrow and I was just . . ."

Elli peered at Charlotte. Her eyes looked a little red—almost as if she'd been crying. *No way,* thought Elli, deciding she must be mistaken. *Not Charlotte.* She focused on the object Charlotte was holding. "But that's not a book, it's—" The words caught in Elli's throat as she realized what Charlotte was holding. "The letters!" she gasped.

"Yes," said Charlotte, smiling grimly. "The letters."

"You read them," Elli whispered.

"Oh, yes, I read them," Charlotte confirmed, with a harsh, unfeeling laugh. "Now we both know. Isn't it astonishing? What a scandal! All those years ago, they had an affair, and now it's started up again."

"I can't believe you're laughing," Elli burst out. "It's no joke. Your father ruined my parents' marriage!"

In a split second, Charlotte's face was transformed. The smile faded; her mouth twisted in a grimace of fury and incalculable pain. "Your mother went further than that," she spat out. "Not only did she ruin *my* parents' marriage, but she killed my mother!"

"What are you talking about?" asked Elli, a chill running up her spine.

"Nine years ago," Charlotte replied ominously, waving the love notes in front of Elli's face. "*Nine years ago.* Don't you know what that means?"

Elli shook her head, frightened and confused.

"The affair," Charlotte continued. "It's why my mother died. It wasn't an accident—you didn't know that, did you? No one knows but me and my father. And your mother. *She* must know very well. She was responsible."

"Your mother *killed* herself?" Elli repeated, the connection between the two events, the death and the affair, slowly dawning. Suddenly another image came back to her. *I was on my bike. Mr. Ransom and Mom were laughing.*

Charlotte ran up, frightened and crying. Elli's heart was banging. *My God, no wonder she's always hated me.*

Charlotte was looking at her through hard, narrow eyes. "Yes, she killed herself. Because my father was in love with another woman. The same woman," she added after a pause, "he's dating now."

9

On Saturday night the yacht club was warm with candlelight and fragrant with banks of fresh flowers. The bejeweled dresses and headpieces of the women sparkled even more brightly than the crystal chandeliers, and the crisp white and pastels of the men's F. Scott Fitzgerald-era costumes provided a softly glowing backdrop. Smoky jazz music wove sensuously through the mild evening air; uniformed staff offered caviar and champagne on silver trays.

But Elli couldn't focus on the beauty and festivity around her. When Chad walked by the house to escort her to the party, it was all she could do to speak—to thank him for the corsage, make small talk. Now, after telling him she had to use the ladies' room, she skulked behind a row of potted palms, desperate for some time alone. Her entire existence, the foundation of her life, had shifted, as if after an earthquake, and she felt shaky, disembodied. *What do I do now?* she wondered. *Should I tell Ethan about the love notes, about the suicide? Who can I talk to?*

Through the fronds of the palms, she watched Ethan and Laura doing the Charleston. Laura was radiant in the pink beaded dress; she'd tucked her hair under the matching cap and as she twirled one of her long necklaces, she looked like a real flapper. Then Elli caught her breath as another young woman entered her field of vision. Charlotte, in the very same dress, her long hair also tamed under a beaded headpiece.

Just like Eliza Chapman and Roxanne Ransom in their matching gowns, Elli thought, remembering the story her grandmother had told in the attic. *Only Laura and Charlotte aren't exactly best buddies.*

"Almost like seeing double, isn't it?" said a voice behind her.

She jumped at the sound. Whirling, she looked up, right into Sam DeWitt's hazel eyes. "Sam. Hi." She felt a now-familiar flush. "Seeing . . . ? Oh, you mean Laura and Charlotte. Yeah, it's freaky."

"So, what do you say?" He placed a hand on her arm, smiling. "I know I'm not famous for being suave on the dance floor, but can I persuade you to attempt the Charleston with me?"

"Oh." Elli felt short of breath. For a brief

moment she had a dazed, scattered recollection of something Laura had told her about Sam, about Sam and Julia not really being serious, about Sam holding out for someone else.

But the conversation had taken place a hundred years ago, in another lifetime. Before the love letters and Charlotte. "Oh, Sam, I—I—" Elli stuttered. "Thanks, but I have to get back to— I have to go." Leaving him staring after her, she darted off, melting into the crowd.

Chad caught up to her before she could escape from the clubhouse. "Elli, I've been looking all over for you!" he exclaimed, grasping her arm. "Come on, let's Charleston."

Elli let him steer her to an open space among the dancing, laughing couples.

"Know that scene in *It's a Wonderful Life* when the dance floor opens up and they all fall in the swimming pool?" Chad asked her. "I've always wanted to try that."

Elli nodded distractedly. She'd learned how to Charleston in a junior-high dance class, so it wasn't hard to go through the motions.

"That was great, huh?" Chad said when the song ended.

"Hmm? Oh, yeah." Elli gave him a small smile.

Chad knitted his brows. Then, without a word, he took Elli's hand and led her outside to the deck. "Something's on your mind," he stated, gazing earnestly into her clouded eyes. "What is it, El?"

141

She turned away from him, looking out over the ink-black water of the cove. Chad was kind, a good listener—but somehow she didn't have the slightest impulse to tell him what was on her mind. "It's nothing I can really put into words," she said lamely.

Now it was his turn to look away. After a moment he cleared his throat nervously. "It's us, isn't it?"

"Us?" Elli repeated. The word sounded strange to her, coming from him. Even after all these weeks, she never thought of them in those terms, as a unit, a pair.

"Our relationship. You're not . . . into it."

"It's not that," she started to protest. "I just—"

"Look, you don't have to pretend," Chad cut in. His mouth twisted in a wry smile. "Believe me, a guy can tell."

Elli bit her lip. A part of her wanted to keep protesting—but she knew she couldn't protect him from the truth any longer. "I'm sorry, Chad. I didn't mean to lead you on."

He forced a laugh. "Hey, it was fun while it lasted."

They stood by the deck railing for several moments in silence. Finally Elli touched his arm. "You should get back inside to the party," she said. "Don't let me ruin your night."

Chad looked into her eyes, his own naked with pain and disappointment. "Sorry to break it to you," he said gruffly, "but it's too late for that." Chad bent swiftly, kissed her cheek, then turned and strode off.

Elli faced the water again, gripping the rail so hard her knuckles whitened. She was alone. What now?

Charlotte put the long ebony cigarette holder to her lips. The cigarette was unlit, but the gesture gave her comfort somehow, confidence.

The party spun around her, a bright, dizzy whirl. Charlotte felt like the cold, dark center of the world, a ball of ice, a stone. Eyes narrowed, she watched her father and Mrs. Wells dance, their bodies close together, mouths laughing, eyes glowing. The sight struck Charlotte like a physical blow. *I knew he was cruel to Mom,* she thought. *She wasn't from a fancy family and she didn't have a college education, so he made her feel inadequate, unimportant. He never had time for her, or for me.* And now the reason was obvious. He'd been unfaithful in body as well as spirit.

Now Charlotte felt the sting of betrayal and rejection that had pushed Annette Ransom to suicide nine years earlier. Charlotte felt a surge of need rise up in her—she was desperate for someone to hold her, whisper in her ear, tell her she was beautiful, worship her, love her. *But not these boys,* she thought disdainfully. Jack, Chip,

Forrest, Tim—she'd been with them all, and they'd been able to satisfy her for only an hour or two. She wanted someone else.

Finally Charlotte saw Laura walking toward the ladies' room with Elli. That meant Ethan was alone.

Charlotte found him in a shadowy corner, away from the lights and dancing, leaning against the wall with a glass in his hand. She slipped up to him from the side, gazing at his handsome profile, at the way the loose white trousers and argyle vest draped his lean form. "Ethan," she whispered, pitching her voice slightly higher, to sound like Laura, "I'm back."

He turned to her and she wrapped her arms around his waist, lifting her face to his for a kiss. He grasped her firmly with his free arm, pulling her close. She pressed her breasts and hips against him, her flesh tingling from the contact, and she felt his body thrill with pleasure. "Laura," he whispered, his eyes burning with desire.

She closed her own eyes so he couldn't see they were blue instead of brown, tangled her fingers in his silky dark hair, and pulled his face to hers, her lips parting in anticipation. He was so close she could feel the warmth of his breath— she could almost taste him. *One kiss,* Charlotte thought, *and he'll never go back to her. One kiss, and he'll be mine again.*

*　　　*　　　*

144

She'd taken him by surprise, sneaking up like that. And as his arms tightened around her and he felt her soft, pliant body, Ethan's surprise and wonder grew. Had Laura ever come to him, reached for him, quite so passionately?

Eyes half shut, he was just a breath away from joining his lips to hers when the scent came to him. This girl was jasmine, honey, and musk, the scents kept simmering by a fierce inner heat. Whereas Laura smelled like a cool lake breeze, berries and vanilla . . .

Ethan jerked back, pushing the girl away from him. "Charlotte! My God," he exclaimed hoarsely. "What in hell do you think you're doing?"

She gazed up at him, her blue eyes burning like stars. "Ethan, I only want to—"

He shook her off, his heart thumping with guilt and fear at how close he'd come to kissing her. "Charlotte, no. *No.*"

Without a backward glance, he ran away from her, praying that no one had seen them, that the palm tree had provided a shield. Ethan searched frantically for Laura and spotted her near the bar with Elli. He started toward her, then stopped again, not trusting his own eyes. How had Charlotte fooled him?

"Ethan, what's the matter?" Laura asked when she saw his expression. "You look like you just saw a ghost."

"It's nothing," he said, trying to stop his body

from shaking. "I just . . . Let's dance. I want to dance with you."

Laughing, Laura shrugged apologetically at Elli and then let Ethan whisk her off to the dance floor. "You're so romantic, sweeping me off my feet like this," she murmured. "What's gotten into you?"

It wasn't a slow song, but Ethan held Laura close, his hands moving from her shoulders down her back to her waist, his face pressed against her hair. "I just wanted to be near you," he whispered. "For a minute, I couldn't remember what this felt like."

She laughed softly. "You're really goofy, do you know that?"

Ethan clutched her more tightly in response. They danced a few more songs, and when they left the dance floor, Ethan stuck to Laura's side like a burr, one arm constantly around her waist. He was afraid to let go of her, to let her out of his sight. He was afraid of his own thoughts, his own powerful memories.

"I can't believe Charlotte's wearing the exact same dress as I am," Laura commented.

"It's much prettier on you," Ethan declared.

"You don't have to say that," she said, sounding pleased. "There's a story behind it, you know. Your grandmother told me and Elli. It turns out that back in the twenties a Chapman girl and a Ransom girl were inseparable best friends."

"Funny," said Ethan.

Laura contemplated Charlotte, who was standing at the other end of the bar with Forrest Madden. "We almost look alike, don't we? I mean, in these dresses. Didn't you do a double take when you first saw her?"

"Maybe just for a second." The guilt washed over him like a wave. *It was dark,* he reasoned, *and the dresses are identical. It's like Laura says—anyone could make the mistake. And I was expecting Laura, so naturally I just assumed it was her.*

But deep inside, he couldn't help questioning his own innocence. Charlotte was his past, Laura was his present and future—the girl he really loved. He should have known the difference immediately. Could Charlotte have fooled him, even for an instant, if he didn't *want* to be fooled?

With a rush of dismay, Elli watched her mother and Mr. Ransom slipping out to the yacht club deck, hand in hand. *Just like last year,* she thought, recalling her own shock, the heated fight between her parents later that night, and her father's abrupt departure. And what about nine years earlier? Had Annette Ransom caught her husband red-handed? Had he sneaked off with Mrs. Wells at that ball too? *Maybe it was Sunday morning, the day after, when she did it,*

147

when she drowned herself, Elli speculated. *She simply couldn't go on any longer.*

When her mother reappeared fifteen minutes later, Elli had made up her mind. She had to say something or she'd explode. She drained her fruit punch, crushing the paper cup in her hand, and then walked toward the bar, where her mother stood with Mr. Ransom. "Mom, I need to talk to you. Alone," she said.

After a brief glance at her companion, Mrs. Wells walked with Elli down a side hallway to a small banquet room. "What's the matter, honey?"

Elli took a deep breath. "I need to know—I need to know about the notes."

"What notes?" asked Mrs. Wells, her forehead wrinkled.

For a brief instant Elli allowed herself to hope, just as she had the previous summer after she saw her mother and Mr. Ransom together. *It's all a mistake,* Elli thought. *The notes . . . maybe he wrote them to her, but it's not how it looks. Maybe he wanted to have an affair, but she wouldn't. She was faithful to Dad—she wouldn't cheat.*

"The notes," Elli said. "Love letters. From Mr. Ransom to you, dated nine summers ago. I—I found them in the attic, in the bottom of a jewelry box."

The color drained from her mother's face, and Elli's hopes drained away with it. Mrs.

Wells stood silently, her lips pressed together.

"Say something!" Elli cried at last.

Her mother shook her head. "What do you want me to say? Apparently you've jumped to a conclusion. Do you want me to defend my actions?"

"You couldn't defend them, not in a million years!" Elli declared hotly. "You told me you and he were just friends, but you're having an affair now and you were having one nine years ago. Did you know Mrs. Ransom killed herself? That when she drowned, it wasn't an accident, it was on purpose? Did you *know* that?"

The color rose in Mrs. Wells's cheeks. "I . . . suspected it."

"And you don't feel the least bit guilty or responsible?" Elli pressed. "That poor, poor woman. And Dad! What you did to *Dad*!"

Mrs. Wells's voice dropped to an agonized whisper. "I— We— We *did* feel guilty. We did feel responsible. After Annette's death, Holling and I stopped seeing each other." Her eyes misted over. "We determined we wouldn't cause any more pain."

Elli's own eyes flooded with tears. "But Mrs. Ransom was *dead.* And Charlotte was motherless. And your marriage to Dad was ruined. Or almost ruined—you finished it off last summer."

"Elli." Mrs. Wells put a hand on her daughter's arm. "I know you're upset, but you have to understand how complicated all this was—is. It's not just black and white. You have to try to see my side of—"

"*Your* side?" Elli shook her head. "You really don't expect me to feel sorry for you, do you?" She shook her head, refusing to let her mother's stricken face affect her. "You don't have a side. Forget it, Mom. Just forget it!"

Before her mother could stop her, Elli ran back down the hall and out the clubhouse door. Her heels sank deep into the lawn and she stumbled, but she didn't slow her pace. *I have to get out of here,* she thought desperately.

As she ran she stepped out of one of her shoes, but she didn't turn back for it. Then someone seized her arm, forcing her to a halt. Elli turned with a gasp. It was Sam.

"Slow down, Elli," he said. "You lost something."

Her arm burned where his fingers touched her. As she looked up at him her breath came even faster. Quickly she yanked her arm away. When he handed her the shoe, she stuck it back on her foot without a word, then turned and started off again, hoping the darkness hid her tears.

"Hold it, Wells," Sam commanded, clutching her arm once more. "Hold it right there. And answer me just this one question: Why do you keep blowing me off?"

Elli stared at him, and all the hurt and confusion she'd been smothering in his presence surged up in her. "*I'm* blowing *you* off? Don't you

150

have it backward, DeWitt? You're the one who's been too busy running after Julia Emerson all summer to spend any time with me!"

"I asked her out only because I never got any encouragement from you," Sam declared, his eyes flashing in the dark. "But there was no point in it, in dating another girl, since you were all I ever thought about anyway."

They stared at each other. Elli remembered again what Laura had told her, about the hints Sam had dropped. She hadn't believed Laura, not really. But these weren't just hints reported secondhand. This was Sam telling her how he felt. This was real. "I didn't know," Elli stammered.

"Julia and I broke up this morning. It just wasn't working," Sam told her. "And I'll wait longer for you if I have to, Elli, but I really don't want to. I mean, I've already waited *years*. Last summer you still didn't seem ready, but this summer I hoped—well, I hoped you were."

Elli felt dizzy. She wanted to laugh and cry at the same time. "I don't know what my problem is. I think about my parents and that whole mess, and I get . . . I don't know. Not scared, but . . . It's just all so . . . ."

"I know how you feel," said Sam. "But you can't be afraid of making mistakes. Taking risks."

Elli gazed into his eyes, hope fluttering in her heart like a caged bird trying to get free. She knew deep down that Sam was right. The world

151

didn't have to end because of what she'd learned about her mother and Mr. Ransom. But the fear was still there. *How can I just let go?* she wondered. *It would be like skydiving . . . without a parachute.* She put a hand to her face. "Oh, Sam," she whispered.

"Elli." Sam spoke her name so softly, it sounded like the voice of the night wind. "Elli, remember last year at the Midsummer Madness ball?"

She nodded, stepping closer. "Do you think . . . do you think we could try it again?" she whispered.

In reply, Sam took her in his arms. Elli shivered with anticipation as she lifted her face to his. They were both taut with the tension of waiting, of holding back, for so long. And then his lips found hers and the tension exploded in a fireworks of fulfillment. Where the kiss the year before had been a question, this kiss was a promise, a new beginning.

Charlotte couldn't stand the sight of Ethan and Laura a single second longer. Forrest had gone to get her a drink, but now she darted from the dance floor without waiting for him to return.

She pushed through the door and the cool night air hit her face. Removing the beaded headpiece, she shook out her hair, then bent to slip off her sandals so she could walk across the lawn barefoot. When she straightened again, she noticed a couple embracing in the moonlight.

At first, watching them, Charlotte felt only a faint curiosity. Who was it? Then she recognized the guy's build—the broad shoulders, the trim waist and hips—and his chestnut hair.

Sam, Charlotte thought.

It took Charlotte a moment to recognize the girl in the glittering gold flapper dress. She was tall and slender with straight, glossy dark hair. It wasn't auburn-haired Julia Emerson. "Elli," Charlotte hissed. Her heart contracted with painful jealousy. Elli and Sam! The one guy Charlotte had always *really* wanted, and now it looked like Elli had her claws in him again.

Charlotte spun around and hurried across the lawn toward Briarwood. No lights were on there—the cottage was dark, loveless, cold. Charlotte stood for a moment on the porch, gazing at the house next door. "Damn them," she cursed, her throat gritty with pent-up tears. "Damn them all." The Wells family always got what they wanted at the expense of others. "But you'll pay for what you've taken from me," Charlotte whispered, her burning eyes still on the house. "You'll pay."

10

Elli slept fitfully, dreams of delirious happiness alternating with blood-chilling nightmares. She woke up at dawn smiling to herself as she remembered what had happened between her and Sam, but her smile faded when she remembered the scene with her mother. *Maybe I should stay in my room for the rest of my life,* Elli thought with a sigh as she sat up in bed and rested her arms on the window sill. The prospect of seeing her mother at the breakfast table was simply too dreadful. How could they go on living in the same house?

Elli took a long, hot shower and then dressed slowly, dragging out the process for as long as possible. Finally, since climbing out the window wasn't an option, she walked slowly downstairs, hoping that Nana or Ethan and Laura were already up.

But when Elli entered the breakfast room, she found only one other person sitting there. "Morning, Mom," she said, her voice almost inaudible.

"Good morning," Mrs. Wells replied stiffly. She blew on her coffee, not looking up at her daughter.

For a moment Elli considered a retreat. But someone had to break the ice, or it would just get colder and colder until they were all frozen solid and unable to make a move toward each other. *And I don't want that,* Elli realized. No matter what had happened, this was still her mother. *And we need each other.*

"Mom." Elli cleared her throat, shifted her weight from one foot to the other. "About last night. I'm . . . I'm sorry. I said some things I should've—I shouldn't have— I'm sorry," she repeated lamely.

A tense silence shivered between them. At last Mrs. Wells put down her coffee cup with a deep sigh. Her posture relaxed slightly. "Me too."

"Well . . ." Elli glanced down the hall at the front door, itching to escape. "I guess I'll head down to the dock. See ya."

"See ya."

It wasn't until she was outside that Elli's guilt and discomfort gave way once more to anger. *Wait a minute,* she thought as she strode toward the lake, planning to walk off her nerves. *Why do I feel sorry? She should be the one apologizing to me!* Then she saw someone waving at her from the beach and all thoughts of her mother instantly disappeared.

They met on the sand, near the edge of the gently lapping lake. "I was hoping you'd be up early," said Sam, a smile lighting his hazel eyes.

"I didn't sleep much," Elli confessed.

"Me either."

Suddenly, in the light of day, they were shy and uncertain. Sam looked away, whistling. Elli dropped her eyes and studied her shoelaces. Then they both started talking at once.

"Sam, I—"

"Elli, what do you say we—"

She laughed. "You first."

"I was going to suggest sneaking off someplace, just the two of us. We have a lot of lost time to make up for, don't you think?"

Elli blushed, her heart pounding. "I like that idea very much."

"Do you?" he asked, his eyes fixed on her face, intent and hopeful. "Do you really? Because last summer, after we . . . you regretted it. You pulled back."

Elli stepped closer. "Not this time," she whispered.

The kiss was even better than the one the night before, full of laughter, as warm and light as sunshine. After, Elli and Sam ran down the beach hand in hand, then cut across the Lowells' lawn to the dock. They rowed a dinghy out to Sam's little sailboat, *Tailgate*. In just a few minutes they were flying across the bright blue water of Lake Michigan, propelled by a fresh morning breeze.

The day passed in a happy blur of romance and discovery. They spent the morning sailing, then docked at Deep River and went into town for lunch. In the afternoon, they returned to Silver Beach, anchoring off Blueberry Island so they could swim to shore and visit the eagles' nest. At sunset, they brought the boat back and hopped in Sam's car, driving to Pentwater for pizza and a movie. It was almost midnight when Sam walked her home.

"I think this has been the longest first date on record," Elli remarked as they sat on the porch steps.

Sam twined her fingers in his. "I wish it didn't have to end."

She smiled at him, her eyes shining in the darkness. "Then how about one more swim?"

Holding hands, they crossed the lawn, wading through the scratchy dune grass. "Remember all our late-night swims last summer?" Sam asked her.

Elli nodded. "I really missed that, when we stopped being friends."

"We were crazy, weren't we?" he said, squeezing her hand.

"Out of our minds," she agreed.

At the lake's edge, they stripped down to their bathing suits, dropping their clothes on the sand. Elli went in up to her knees, her thighs, her waist. Then she dove. When she surfaced, Sam was right beside her. "So, tell me," he said, floating on his back. "Josh what's-his-name back in Winnetka. Is that serious? I mean, do I have competition?"

Elli laughed. "Poor Josh. I forgot all about him. No, we weren't that serious. I mean, we went out for a while, but it wasn't . . ." *It wasn't like this.*

"But you made it sound like you were still going out with him."

"I guess I wanted you to think . . ." Elli flushed, embarrassed. "Here you are, this older guy, this *college* guy," she teased. Sam splashed her. "I just wanted you to think I'd . . . grown up."

Sam laughed ruefully. "Yeah, well, instead I thought you were trying to tell me to get lost."

They swam back into the shallows and Elli reached for Sam. "We have it all straightened out now, though, don't we?"

"I'm feeling pretty good about it, yeah," he agreed, his voice husky.

They stood in the lake, arms clasped around each other's waists, water streaming down their bodies. "Let's pretend it's the first night of summer," Elli whispered. "Before Julia, before Chad. And you came down to my end of the beach and found me here and . . ."

"And kissed you before you had a chance to talk me out of it." Sam smoothed the damp hair back from her forehead. "And we had all summer ahead of us."

She heard the regret in his voice. "Don't think about the time we wasted," she urged. "Think about the time we still have left." Her lips curved in an inviting smile; her eyes sparkled with promises. "Because summer's not over yet, Sam DeWitt."

"I can't believe it," Ethan exclaimed as he and Elli ate lunch on the porch of the cottage. Laura was sunbathing out of earshot. "Mom and Mr. Ransom were having an affair nine years ago? And Charlotte's mother found out about it and killed herself?"

"I know—it's terrible," Elli said gloomily.

Ethan wrapped his arms around his knees, his eyes on Briarwood. "Poor Charlotte," he muttered. Maybe that explains why . . ."

"Why what?" asked Elli when he didn't complete the sentence.

Ethan flushed slightly. He couldn't tell her about the trick Charlotte had played at the ball, and how close he'd come to falling for it. "Nothing. I mean, maybe it explains . . . maybe it explains how wild she's acting these days. Partying all night with that bad Pentwater crowd." He stuck his hand in the bag of potato chips. "She's acting out, looking for something. A girl as sensitive as Charlotte would—"

Elli burst out laughing. "I'm sorry, Ethan. But *Charlotte,* sensitive? She was as hard as nails when she told me about it. It was vintage Charlotte—ice cold, totally biting and nasty."

"But that could just be a cover for her real feelings," Ethan argued. "You don't *know* Charlotte, Elli."

She looked away without responding, and Ethan's last statement hung in the air. He wondered if Elli was thinking the same thing he was. How many times during the previous summer had he defended his love for Charlotte to Elli with just those words—"You don't know what she's really like"?

"I feel sorry for Charlotte," Elli said after a moment. "I really do." She directed a pointed glance at Laura, stretched out on a beach towel on the grass. "But take my advice. Don't let feeling sorry for her cloud your judgment."

"Of course not," Ethan replied.

My judgment is rock solid, Ethan told himself later that day as he walked toward Briarwood. Sam, Elli, and Laura were taking a sunset sail on the *Silver Dollar;* Ethan had stayed behind, claim-

160

ing he'd promised his grandmother he'd give her a hand with some things around the house.

He bumped into Charlotte on her way out of the cottage. She was wearing a clingy scoop-necked knit top and a long gauzy skirt that distinctly showed the shape of her legs. "Got a hot date?" he asked, fighting down an unexpected flare of jealousy.

Charlotte narrowed her eyes. "Yeah, as a matter of fact I do."

She started to brush past him. Ethan put a hand on her arm. "I know you're on your way someplace, but can I talk to you? It'll just take a minute."

Charlotte stood in front of him, her arms folded, and stared boldly into his face. "About what?"

Ethan glanced over his shoulder. He didn't want anyone to see them together. "Let's go inside," he suggested.

Charlotte hesitated, then shrugged. "Okay," she agreed, turning around and walking back up the porch steps, "but don't make me late."

He followed her into the living room. Charlotte sat down on the sofa and crossed her legs. Ethan perched on an easy chair. "Go ahead," she said.

Ethan cleared his throat. "It's about the other night."

"Oh, that." Charlotte laughed carelessly. "I was just playing games with you, Ethan. I hope you're not bent out of shape about it."

"No, of course not." He cleared his throat. "I was . . . confused. Just for a minute. But I think I understand."

She tipped her head to one side. "Understand what?"

"You. Elli told me," he explained. "About the letters. About what really happened to your mom."

Charlotte blushed, ever so slightly. "I don't see what this has to do with anything," she said with a harsh laugh. "If you're here to apologize to me on behalf of your family or something like that, it's a little late. A little pointless."

Ethan shook his head. "I don't want to talk about our parents. I just wanted you to know that I'm still— I know we have a . . . past, but I'm still your friend. And I'm worried about you."

He spit out the last words and braced himself for some of her mocking laughter. But instead Charlotte's pretty face crumpled. Slender shoulders hunched, she buried her face in her hands and began to sob.

Ethan dashed over to the sofa and sat down beside her, slipping an arm around her. "Char, I didn't mean to make you cry. Please, Char. Stop crying. It's okay. I'm here. I want to help."

She looked up at him through a curtain of tumbled honey-blond hair, her blue eyes huge and bright with tears. "Really? You really want to help me?"

"Really," Ethan swore. "Like I said, I'm your friend."

"Then kiss me," she whispered, bringing her face close to his.

Ethan could feel the warmth of her body beneath the thin shirt and skirt; like the other night at the ball, he could smell her natural, intoxicating perfume. He stiffened. "That's not what I meant by help," he said. "And it wouldn't. Help, I mean."

She pressed closer, her hand on his knee. "How do you know if you don't try, Ethan? Maybe it's what we both need. You've been restless lately, too. I can sense it."

He shook his head firmly, though her observation had struck a nerve. "I'm not restless. I'm happy. I love Laura."

Once again, Charlotte's eyes brimmed with tears. "But you used to love me. Didn't you?"

"Yes," Ethan replied, looking away from her. "But that was a long time ago."

"I don't believe it," she cried. "You can't just stop loving someone, if you really loved them in the first place. And I won't ever believe . . ." Her hand slid up his thigh. "I'll never believe," she whispered, "that you care more for her than you do for me. That you feel the same passion. Admit it, Ethan. It pales in comparison. You want more. You need more. And I can give it to you."

She was so close. Her lips touched the pulse point in his throat, moved up to his jaw. Ethan felt the heat rise in his body in response. His eyes blurred, and for a moment, in a wave of rekindled desire, he forgot everything and everyone but Charlotte.

Then he grasped Charlotte's arms and shoved her away. "Stop it, Charlotte," he commanded hoarsely. "Stop right there."

"Why, Ethan?" She leaned close again, pleading. "Why shouldn't we go back to the way we—"

"Because it's wrong," he broke in, giving her a shake. "It was wrong then and it's wrong now. It could never be right between us, Char, ever again."

She turned her face away. He watched her struggle for control, gulp back the tears. When at last she spoke, her voice was as cold and sharp as steel. "Get out of my house, Ethan Wells."

Ethan dropped his hands from her arms and rose to his feet. "I'm sorry," he said in a voice that sounded faraway to his own ears. "Goodbye, Charlotte."

"I heard you lovebirds are having dinner at Eagle Point tonight," Charlotte remarked with a snide glance at Elli the next day, popping a piece of bubble gum in her mouth. The girls were sitting on the edge of the dock, watching their campers sail around the cove. "So you're officially a couple at last."

"I guess we are," Elli replied stiffly.

Charlotte laughed. "Don't get pissy. I'm just

164

jealous. I mean, *you* snagged Sam DeWitt. The most gorgeous guy in Silver Beach, the grand prize, the brass ring." A trace of bitterness crept into her voice. "Elli Wells gets lucky again."

Elli shrugged. Charlotte snapped her gum, studying the other girl's cool, aristocratic profile. *Elli Wells gets lucky again, and I get . . . nothing.*

Absolutely nothing, Charlotte added to herself as she remembered her encounter with Ethan the day before. Elli was probably behind Ethan's resistance, Charlotte decided. Elli had always hated the idea of her perfect brother dating Charlotte, and she'd probably encouraged him to bring dull Laura to Silver Beach—anything to keep Ethan and Charlotte apart.

"Do you ever think about fate?" Charlotte asked.

Elli shot her a quizzical glance. "Fate? In what way?"

"You know, destiny. Life as a wheel—what goes around, comes around. That sort of thing."

"Not really." For a moment Elli gazed intently out at the campers on the lake. Then she looked at Charlotte again. "Why, do you?"

Charlotte nodded. "You see, I believe in fate, in destiny. Take your mom and my dad, for example. Fate brought them together, fate drove my mother into the lake. But one of these days they'll be punished."

Elli shuddered. "Do you have to be so ghoulish, Charlotte?"

"And Ethan," Charlotte continued. "We were meant for each other, ever since childhood. And someday we'll get back together."

"That's where you're definitely wrong," Elli declared. "He's serious about Laura. You'll never break them up."

"And you," Charlotte continued, ignoring Elli's assertion. She fixed Elli with a steady, speculative gaze. "You have it all, don't you? It's always been like that. You win every race you enter—you're everybody's favorite. You have a great brother who has a great girlfriend and maybe your parents are getting divorced, but your mom's working on landing you a pretty decent stepdad. A Pulitzer–prize-winning novelist! And Sam is the icing on the cake. But you shouldn't get too cocky." She stood up, looming over Elli. "Because fate won't let you have all the luck forever. And the more you have to lose . . ." She let the sentence dangle, delighting in the dread forming on Elli's face. "And as for me," she concluded in a whisper, "I have nothing to lose. Keep that in mind."

With a critical eye, Theodore DeWitt surveyed the long mahogany table in the opulent dining room at Eagle Point. Set with crystal, silver, and formal china, the table looked pretty nice to Sam, but he could tell that his handsome, white-haired grandfather felt something was still missing. "Flowers," Mr. DeWitt said at last. "Go out in the garden and pick some, son. Roses—a big armful. Eleanor loves them."

"I can't believe we're fussing this much," Sam kidded. "It's not like we're hosting the Queen of England. Mrs. Chapman comes over here all the time."

"But not for *dinner,*" Mr. DeWitt pointed out, looking shocked at his grandson's ignorance of social etiquette. "And not with daughter and granddaughter in tow. I consider this a very special occasion."

With a grin, Sam went out to the garden to clip some roses. After sticking them in a crystal bowl in the center of the dining room table, he joined his grandfather in the kitchen. Mr. DeWitt was mumbling the menu to himself. "Chilled fresh tomato and corn soup—already done and in the fridge. Poached salmon with dill sauce, *haricots verts*, new potatoes . . . and wine. Hmm. Must make a trip down to the cellar."

"Relax, Grandpa," said Sam, lounging against the counter and popping the top on a can of soda. "They won't be here for an hour. We have plenty of time."

Mr. DeWitt smiled. "You're right. No reason to get in such a dither. It's just that ordinarily you and I lead such a bachelor's life at Eagle Point in the summer. My culinary skills are reduced to steaks on the grill."

"Don't get me wrong," said Sam. "This is a nice idea, having Elli and Mrs. Wells and Mrs. Chapman over. Elli." He repeated the name, shaking his head in happy disbelief. "I guess I never really imagined it could be like this."

"You like this girl, eh?" his grandfather observed.

Sam nodded. "Yeah. She's . . ." He searched for the words, but his vocabulary seemed woefully inadequate. "Terrific. But I should probably tell you, just so you know, things are kind of tense between her and her mom these days. I'm not even sure they're talking to each other."

"Hmm," Theodore DeWitt murmured knowingly. "She's upset about her mother dating another man, is that it?"

"Yeah, but it's not just that she's dating him. It turns out this affair goes back a long time."

"A long time." Mr. DeWitt nodded. "So Elli found out. Yes, a long time indeed."

Sam raised an eyebrow, suddenly aware of the history his grandfather was privy to. "You know all about it, don't you? I mean, people must have talked back then. It's hard to keep a secret for long in a place like this."

"Very hard," his grandfather agreed. "But Holling and Grace . . . no, that was never common knowledge."

"Still, maybe the big surprise is that it took this

long for Elli to find out the truth," Sam commented. "That her mother was seeing Mr. Ransom nine years ago."

Mr. DeWitt shot a sharp glance at Sam. "Nine years?"

"You mean you didn't know? Yeah, nine years. Must've started up at the beginning of the summer. Then Mrs. Ransom caught on and . . . well, you know what happened to her. It turns out it was suicide."

Mr. DeWitt still looked startled.

"What?" said Sam. "Is there another version of the story?"

"No, no," Mr. DeWitt replied. "Not another version exactly."

"What, then?" asked Sam. "Isn't this the whole story?" A wary light flickered in his grandfather's eyes, and immediately Sam knew he'd stumbled onto something. "It's not the whole story. There's more, isn't there?"

After a long pause, Mr. DeWitt nodded slowly. "Yes, there is. Much more." He turned away from his grandson. "I think I'll go choose the wine. Why don't you see if there are guest towels in the powder room?"

"Grandpa!" Sam declared. "You can't just walk away after that."

"I shouldn't have spoken," Mr. DeWitt replied. "Some things are better left unsaid."

"You have to tell me what you know," Sam

insisted. "I care about Elli, and if this concerns her . . . *Does* it concern her?"

Mr. DeWitt shook his head. "This knowledge I have . . . it isn't mine. I don't own it."

"I only want to protect Elli," said Sam. "You can trust me."

For what felt like an eternity, Mr. DeWitt studied his grandson's face. Then, apparently having come to a decision, he drew a deep breath. He uttered three sentences, his voice low, even, unemotional.

Sam stared at his grandfather, stunned and speechless. "I trust you to be responsible with this," Mr. DeWitt concluded, placing a firm hand on Sam's arm. "Discreet. Before you say anything to young Miss Wells, think carefully about what you mean when you say you want to protect her."

Mr. DeWitt left the kitchen, and Sam heard footsteps descending into the basement. He sank back against the counter, his head spinning. It had been wild enough to learn that Mrs. Wells and Mr. Ransom had been having an affair nine years before, an affair that drove Mrs. Ransom to suicide, an affair that ended the Wellses' marriage when it was rekindled years later. But this secret was so dark, so shocking. *It's like a bomb,* Sam thought, *ticking silently all these years.* If it exploded, it would rock Silver Beach like an earthquake. It would destroy Elli's world. "She can't ever know," Sam whispered. His grandfather was right. Some secrets were better left buried. Elli must never, ever find out the whole horrible truth.

11

"The last day of camp—how'd it sneak up on us so soon?"

Charlotte bristled at the sound of Laura's sugary-voiced remark to Ethan. The couple was standing knee-deep at the water's edge, and Charlotte was watching them through her sunglasses.

"That's summer for you," Ethan replied. "When you're a kid, it seems to last forever, but the older you get, the faster it goes."

Traditionally, there were no formal activities on the last day of camp—just games and awards for campers and counselors alike. At that moment, Sam and Elli were at one end of the beach organizing the little kids into a tug of war. Meanwhile, at the other end, the counselors were pairing up boy-girl for a giant game of chicken.

Charlotte kept one eye and ear on Ethan and

Laura. "The faster it goes," Laura agreed with a sigh, resting her head on Ethan's shoulder. "We'll be going home in a week. But I'll never forget Silver Beach. Thanks for bringing me here."

"It was my best summer ever," Ethan told her.

Charlotte stifled the urge to gag.

"Be my partner, Char?" Chip Branford asked, wading up to her.

Charlotte pried her eyes away from the happy couple and was pleased to find Chip looking particularly delectable in faded blue swim trunks and a deep end-of-summer tan. She rewarded him with a brilliant smile. "You bet."

Charlotte climbed onto Chip's broad shoulders. Chip grasped her knees; Charlotte tucked her ankles around his waist. She was glad to see that Ethan and Laura were on the other team. *Maybe I'll get a chance to dunk her,* she thought with a sly smile.

"This isn't really chicken in its purest form," Chip grunted as a Nerf football was thrown into the water by the referee. The two teams began to splash around in hot pursuit. "More like water polo."

"Right," said Charlotte, stretching her arms high. "Over here!" she called to Heather. "I'm open!"

Heather lobbed the ball and Charlotte caught the pass. Pivoting, Chip barreled through the water, aiming for the goal. As Amber and Chad, on the opposite team, got dangerously near,

Charlotte spiraled the Nerf to Becky, who was riding on Doug's shoulders.

Doug galloped to the goal and scored. Becky, Charlotte, and the rest of their team shrieked and hollered.

"Maybe it's not real chicken, but it's fun," Charlotte said to Chip as they moved into position for the next tossup.

"Yep," he agreed. "I mean, this is about as wild as it gets in safe old Silver Beach. What can you expect?"

"Not a whole lot," Charlotte murmured. Something about Chip's comment struck her to the core. *Not real chicken. About as wild as it gets.* Real games of chicken were certainly wild contests. *Like powerboat chicken,* Charlotte thought. *I haven't played that in years.* Her eyes gleamed with sudden inspiration. *No, I haven't played that in years, but maybe it's time.*

"Last night was fun," Elli said to Sam as they stood in line for burgers at the last-day-of-camp picnic lunch. "But you were kind of quiet at dinner. Was it weird having us over?"

"Not at all," Sam was quick to assure her. He gave her a rakish smile. "I just didn't feel like I could compete with all you sparkling conversationalists."

"Yeah, right." Elli laughed. "The topics were pretty sexy. Let's see . . . Gardening? We spent at least forty minutes talking about fertilizing rosebushes. And birdwatching. That got the witty remarks flying."

"Nice pun," Sam groaned.

"Did you say nice buns?" Ethan asked as he and Laura came up behind them. "Watch your mouth around my sister, mister."

"Yes, sir," Sam replied, wrapping an arm around Elli.

When their paper plates were loaded with hamburgers, chips, pickles, and fruit, Elli, Sam, Ethan, and Laura staked out a spot on the yacht club lawn in the shade of a birch tree. "Here's to the end of a great summer," Laura toasted, lifting her soda can.

"Actually, this isn't the end," Sam told her. "The last week after camp wraps up is the best time." He smiled meaningfully at Elli. "Total freedom."

"Everybody goes wild," Ethan agreed. "Parties every night."

"Did someone say party? Where? When?"

Elli turned to find Charlotte standing over the group and smiling at each of the four in turn.

"Mind if I join you?" Charlotte asked.

Elli glanced at Ethan, who glanced at Laura. Laura dropped her eyes, studying the food on her plate with sudden interest. "Uh, no. Sure. Sit down," Ethan invited.

Elli and Sam exchanged uncomfortable glances.

"So," said Charlotte cheerfully. "It was fun

teaching sailing with Elli, but I can't say I'm sorry camp's over. Finally I get to sleep in."

"Next summer, teach water-skiing," Sam recommended. "You get the other counselor to drive and then you can lounge in the back of the boat and be the spotter. Most of the kids are pretty good, so it's safe to doze off."

Charlotte laughed. "Thanks for the tip."

Elli nibbled on her french fries, still waiting for Charlotte to come out with something nasty. *Maybe about Mom and her father,* she thought uneasily. *She must hate it as much as we do, but she loves twisting the knife.* Elli glanced at Ethan. He sat straight and stiff, as though braced for a blow. Meanwhile Laura shrank into herself, her shoulders hunched and her eyes downcast. Elli frowned. Six weeks earlier, when they first arrived at Silver Beach, Laura had been brimming with confidence around Charlotte, laughing off any threat she might represent. What had happened since then?

"I always get nostalgic at the end of summer, you know?" Charlotte mused, snapping a dill pickle spear in two. "I think back to all the good times I've had at Silver Beach in the past."

Here it comes, thought Elli. *She's going to say something disgustingly personal and inappropriate to embarrass Ethan and Laura.*

"Like Hugh's thirteenth birthday party," Charlotte went on. "Remember that? We all packed onto the Lowellses' paddleboat and then we had that giant cake fight."

"Everybody jumped in the cove in their clothes to clean off," Elli told Laura, relieved at Charlotte's neutral comment but also a little wary.

"And the summer it rained nonstop for two weeks," Charlotte continued. "What were we, about ten? The camp counselors were going nuts trying to keep us amused and then Gil Madden showed up at the clubhouse with his black-and-white slides from the old days at Silver Beach, and his World War Two medals and stuff."

"He just started telling stories," Sam recalled, "and we were all hypnotized. It was totally fascinating. When the sun finally came out, we didn't want to go back outside."

"We did some nutty things," said Charlotte, shaking her head and smiling. She looked at Ethan. "Remember when I dared you to walk the yacht club roof in that thunderstorm?"

"I remember, all right," he said with a grin.

"And playing chicken with powerboats," she added.

Ethan laughed. "We'd go out at night. Man, that was crazy!" He turned to Laura. "I *always* chickened out first. Charlotte won every time."

"And Mom and Dad would kill you when they found out," Elli reminded Ethan.

"It was worth it, though, wasn't it?" asked Charlotte, her eyes sparkling. "I mean, there's nothing like getting in trouble for a good reason. We really had a blast."

"It was kind of a kick," Ethan agreed.

"You know, I think we all could use some of that old-fashioned excitement in our lives," Charlotte declared brightly. "How about a game of powerboat chicken tonight, the five of us? Like the old days, just for laughs?"

Elli shook her head. "It's not the safest game, Charlotte."

"Oh, come on," Charlotte wheedled. "No one ever got hurt. What do you say, Laura? Doesn't it sound like fun?"

Laura looked far from certain. "Powerboats? After dark? I'm not sure—"

"You guys aren't going to wimp out on me, are you?" Charlotte said to Sam and Ethan.

"Well . . ." Sam began.

"Let's do it," Ethan said suddenly. "We'll have a good time." He gave Laura an encouraging smile.

For a split second Laura glanced at Charlotte. Then she looked at Ethan and returned his smile. "I guess—I guess it could be fun."

Charlotte beamed triumphantly. "There! So what do you two wimps say? You wouldn't want to miss out on the fun, would you? Come on, for old times' sake?"

Sam chuckled softly. "It *was* pretty exciting, playing chicken in the old days."

Elli tried to smile back at him, but she felt her

stomach knot. In Silver Beach, a dare was a dare and once you accepted, you had to go through with it. What had they just gotten themselves into?

Sam approached Elli's house late in the afternoon, swinging a tennis racket and whistling. He and Elli had a tennis date. And he still couldn't quite believe it. They were acting casual and comfortable about being a couple, but every now and then he still found himself dumbstruck with amazement. *Me and Elli. Elli and me. Finally.*

Hearing voices on the other side of the porch, Sam rounded the corner. Elli was chatting with Mr. Ransom, and looking vaguely uncomfortable.

Recalling his grandfather's revelation, Sam turned pale, but Elli smiled at him with relief. "Sam, hi," she said. "I'm almost ready—just have to run inside and get my racket."

Elli ran into the house, and Sam tried to compose his expression. "Hi, Mr. Ransom. How's the book coming along?"

"Just fine," Mr. Ransom replied. He glanced at his wristwatch. "And I should be getting back to the cottage—I'm expecting a call from my agent."

"See you around."

Mr. Ransom was halfway across the lawn to Briarwood when Elli returned to the porch. She caught Sam staring after him. "Hey, you look a little

179

spooked," she observed. "What's the matter?"

"The matter?" Once again Sam tried to look innocent. He twirled his racket. "Nothing's the matter."

Elli cocked her head to one side. "Are you weirded out that I was talking to Mr. Ransom?"

Sam cleared his throat. "Well, it is kind of surprising."

Elli nodded. "I know. Believe me, I'd avoid him if I could. But it's kind of hard, seeing as how he's my neighbor *and* my mother's boyfriend."

"Yeah. Right," Sam replied awkwardly.

Elli studied his face. "Something's on your mind; it's obvious. Want to tell me about it?"

Sam shook his head and started down the steps.

"What do you mean?" asked Elli, chasing after him. "No, you don't have anything on your mind, or no, you don't want to tell me?"

"Nothing's on my mind," Sam told her, knowing he had no choice but to lie.

"You can't fool me, Sam. There *is* something," she pressed. "You can tell me."

"It's nothing, all right?" Sam replied. "Can we just drop it?"

Elli bit her lip. "Sorry. I was only trying to—I just thought at this point we could trust each other."

"I do trust you," said Sam. "And if I had something to say, I'd say it. Let's not make a mountain out of a molehill, okay?"

They walked to the tennis courts in awkward silence, Sam kicking himself for being so transparent. It had taken Elli about one second flat to figure out he was keeping something from her. *I'll really have to watch myself,* he thought grimly, *if I don't want her to guess that I know something about her family that she doesn't. Something big.*

"Hey, you're not mad at me, are you?" he asked, putting an arm around her shoulders.

She slipped her arm around his waist. "Of course not."

"Our first fight," he kidded.

"It wasn't *really* a fight," she pointed out.

"Let's not ever have a real fight, then."

"We won't," replied Elli. "Not if we're always honest with each other."

Sam nodded. "Right," he said.

Laura and Elli stood at the kitchen counter, making a big salad for supper. The radio was on and Elli was humming along. After a moment Laura reached over and turned down the volume. "Elli," she said tentatively.

"Umm?"

"About tonight. This powerboat chicken thing."

Elli chopped a red bell pepper in half and started scraping out the seeds. "What about it?"

"The way you play it. Two people drive their boats straight at each other and whoever turns away first loses. Right?"

Elli grimaced. "Sounds insane, doesn't it?"

"I'm not really looking forward to it," Laura confessed. "I mean, I'd be lying if I said it was my idea of fun."

"Only a crazy person like Charlotte would actually think it's fun," Elli said. "The rest of us are just going along with her. God knows why."

"Because Ethan wants to," Laura murmured.

"Look, don't worry about it," said Elli. "You don't have to play if you don't want. You can watch from the dock. It's just a silly Silver Beach thing."

Laura pictured herself sitting on the dock while Sam and Elli raced one boat and Ethan and Charlotte raced another. It didn't help to remind herself that it wouldn't matter to Ethan, that he'd been more attentive lately—somehow the image was more than she could bear.

"I want to be part of Silver Beach, though," said Laura. "I don't want to be left out. I—I think I'll play."

"Only if you want to," Elli reiterated. "It's your choice. Seriously. It's no big deal one way or another."

It's my choice. No big deal, Laura thought. But she couldn't help sensing that it *was* a big deal. Something was at stake. "I'll play," she repeated, mustering a smile. "I'll race with Ethan, and we'll win."

12

By sunset, Elli was having second thoughts of her own. After helping her grandmother with the supper dishes, she hunted down her brother. Ethan was slumped on the family room couch with his feet on the coffee table, channel-surfing. "Is Laura around?" Elli asked him.

"Upstairs," replied Ethan. "Taking a shower."

Elli crossed the room and sat down next to him. "Ethan, I've been thinking about . . . Charlotte's proposition." She lowered her voice so no one could hear her from the hallway. "I know nobody's ever gotten hurt in the past, but maybe we shouldn't do this."

Ethan pointed the remote control at the TV. "It's just a game, Elli."

"Potentially a really dangerous one. Let's call it off."

He gave her the same answer she'd given Laura

earlier. "You don't have to play if you don't want."

"I don't think any of us should play. Laura's not psyched and neither am I. So what's the point?"

Ethan shrugged, still staring straight ahead at the TV. "Like Charlotte said, it's just for kicks."

"I thought you were past the stage of jumping at every suggestion Charlotte makes," said Elli, sarcasm creeping into her voice.

"I'm not jumping at anything," Ethan shot back. "Look, like I said, you don't have to come out tonight. But Laura explicitly told me she wants to play, so quit trying to ruin the fun for everyone else."

Elli studied her brother's profile. This stubbornness—she hadn't seen it since the previous summer. The summer of Charlotte. *Something's going on between the two of them,* Elli thought. *It's one of Charlotte's dares—it's some kind of test.* The old impulse to protect Ethan from Charlotte rose up, prodding her. She knew she could sit out, but somehow the idea of *not* being there to keep an eye on things seemed more dangerous than the game itself.

Elli got reluctantly to her feet. Ethan was the only one with the power to call the whole thing off, and clearly he wasn't going to change his mind. As she turned to leave the room a wave of fear washed over her—a shapeless, dark premonition. "I just hope we don't regret this," she whispered.

"What?" asked Ethan.

"Nothing," said Elli.

She read in her room until eleven-thirty, then crept downstairs. Her mother and grandmother were in bed; Ethan and Laura were watching TV together.

She and Sam had arranged to meet fifteen minutes early on the beach. Elli took the path to the dunes. In the black, moonless night, she could barely distinguish between the lake and the beach. "Sam?" Elli called, uncertain.

He took a step in her direction, a shadow detaching from the other shadows. "Over here."

Elli moved toward him, and they stumbled into each other. She laughed as he wrapped his arms around her. "Sure it's you?" she asked. "I can't even see your face. For all I know, I'm hugging a stranger."

"I'm not strange," said Sam in a deep, Dracula-esque voice.

She laughed again, then pulled away from him slightly. "So. Do you want to take a walk?"

Sam brushed her cheek with a kiss. "I kind of like it right here."

Elli's whole body tingled as his lips traveled down her jawbone to the corner of her mouth, but at the same time, she felt tense. As close as she was to him, she felt oddly detached, separate. Something as shadowy as the night seemed to wedge itself between them. *Our disagreement this afternoon?* she wondered distractedly. *Or am I just worried about what we're all about to do?*

"Sam." Elli pushed against his chest, looking up into his face. She could discern his features now that her eyes had adjusted to the dark. "Let's not . . ." She didn't know what she wanted to say. *Let's not kiss right now? Let's not play powerboat chicken?* "Let's go," she said at last. "It's time to meet the others."

Ethan led Laura down the dock, holding her hand. Laura tripped over an uneven board and nearly fell. He stopped to steady her. "You all right?"

"Yeah," she said somewhat breathlessly. "But . . . are you sure this is . . . I mean, how are we going to see? You said we can't use the lights on the boats because we'll get in trouble if we get caught."

"Don't worry, we'll be able to see, or *hear,* anyway." He gave her a playful squeeze. "Really is dark, isn't it? But, hey, that just makes it even more fun."

Laura wasn't convinced, but she kept her doubts to herself. They continued along the dock, their sneakers slapping on the wood. At the end, she could make out three dim forms— Charlotte, Elli, and Sam.

"So, we're all here," said Charlotte in greeting. "Nobody's chickened out . . . yet."

Ethan laughed. "I'm warning you, Ransom—I'm tougher than I used to be."

Laura saw a flash of white—Charlotte smiling widely. "We'll see about that, Wells."

"Whose boats are we going to take?" asked Sam.

"I'd offer mine, but I just remembered it's out of gas," said Charlotte. "Okay if we use yours, Sam? And yours, Ethan?"

"Fine with me," said Ethan.

"Elli and I will go in my boat," said Sam.

"And Laura and I will take our boat," said Ethan. "Why don't you come with us, Char?"

Laura grit her teeth. *Char,* she repeated to herself. It sounded so familiar, so affectionate. *I don't want her in the boat with me.*

"Well? What do you say?" Ethan pressed.

For an endless moment Charlotte stared at Laura, her eyes gleaming in the dark. Then she shook her head. "No, thanks," she said. "I think I'll ride with Sam and Elli. If that's okay with you guys."

Elli shrugged.

"Sure," said Sam.

"Then let's get started," Charlotte said brightly.

Ethan strode over to his family's Boston Whaler, Laura close on his heels. When he stopped to untie the line from the cleat, she ran right into him, almost knocking him off the dock into the water. "Watch it!" he cried.

Laura heard Charlotte's tinkling laugh behind

her and felt her cheeks heat up. "Sorry," she muttered.

When the boat was untied, Ethan helped Laura in, then climbed in himself. He started the motor, letting it idle on low, and left the running lights off.

The sound of Sam's motor resounded across the still water. "Someone's bound to hear us," said Laura, a hopeful note in her voice. "Maybe we shouldn't do this."

Ethan twisted the handle that acted as both tiller and throttle, revving the engine and drowning her out. He steered into the cove. The Whaler carved through the dark water, sending up a ghostly wake. Pushing her wind-tossed hair from her eyes, Laura turned to look at Sam's boat, which had pulled up alongside them. Sam wasn't at the wheel.

"I'm driving," Charlotte called to them. Another white smile flashed across her face—challenging, taunting. *And that smile is aimed at me,* thought Laura, a kernel of fear sprouting in her stomach. *She keeps looking at me.* "We'll be seeing you," Charlotte added. "And may the best man . . . or woman . . . win."

Charlotte steered Sam's boat to the east side of the cove. Motoring slowly toward the opposite shore, Ethan glanced at Laura out of the corner of his eye. She was silent, her gaze fixed dead ahead. He could feel her fear, and he knew he should say something to reassure her, but the words stuck in his throat. *How many times do I have to tell her to chill out, that this is just a game?* he thought, suppressing a prick of annoyance. *She's a big girl—I shouldn't have to baby her.*

When they were nearly at Blueberry Island, Ethan swung the Whaler in a wide arc so they were facing the middle of the cove. He let the motor idle and flashed his lights briefly. From the far side of the cove came an answering flash. Then the night was black again except for a tiny speck of white. "Elli's handkerchief," Laura whispered. "The signal."

Ethan kept his eyes glued to the white spot, counting down silently. *Three, two, one . . .* The handkerchief swept downward. Laura drew in her breath. Across the cove, an engine roared. Turning the throttle full force, Ethan sent the Whaler flying forward. The game had begun.

As the boat skimmed across the surface of the water, light and swift as a bird, Ethan felt his body flood with adrenalin. It was like the old days, when Charlotte used to dare him. *Then it was just her and me,* he remembered, *or me and Elli against her and some guy, some boyfriend.* And it was true, what he'd told the others at lunch—Charlotte won every time.

But not tonight, Ethan determined, bending

his head, his eyes watering from the wind. As a boy, he'd always turned away first, and Charlotte taunted him for his cowardice. But now he felt, vaguely, that he had to prove something to her—and to Laura, and to himself.

Dimly he saw the other boat speeding toward him. Laura's fear enveloped him—he knew that for her sake he should play it safe, turn aside, accept defeat—but he kept his own boat pointing forward. *I'm not turning. She'll turn aside first. She has to.* The thought turned into a prayer. *Turn, Charlotte. Please.*

Charlotte laughed into the wind, shaking her hair recklessly. "Isn't this great?" she shouted to Elli and Sam. "Watch him. He's going to turn, any second."

Elli and Sam were crouched low in the boat, their faces tense and unsmiling. *And Laura's cowering, too,* Charlotte thought with infinite pleasure. *I'll show her she doesn't belong here. I'll show them all who's still in charge at Silver Beach.*

She could see Ethan's boat clearly now. "Charlotte, slow down," Elli cried. "He's not going to turn."

"He'll turn," Charlotte said with confidence. "He always does."

But he was going farther than he ever had before. She could see the pale blur of his face, of Laura's face. *Well, aren't you a brave little boy,*

Charlotte thought, amused. *Trying to scare me, are you?* But he'd turn—of course he'd turn. He always turned, and then he'd have to acknowledge her strength, his weakness.

Charlotte gripped the wheel, her jaw set. "Turn!" Elli begged.

"No!" she shouted back.

Now she could see the whites of Ethan's eyes, his face as fixed and determined as her own. A thrill of fear pulsed through Charlotte's veins. Sam was yelling now. "Turn, goddamnit, *turn!*"

At the last possible moment Ethan yanked his arm, swinging the tiller violently to the side. The Whaler swerved, bucking. Charlotte too spun the wheel, but not sharply enough. Her boat rammed into the side of his, just at the point where Laura was sitting. Over the sound of splintering fiberglass, as her own body was flung into the water by the impact, Charlotte heard a high-pitched scream. *Laura,* she thought.

Elli clawed her way to the surface of the water, gasping for air and sobbing. "Sam! Sam!"

He reached her side with a few quick strokes. "Elli, are you all right?"

"I—I think so," she sputtered. The crumpled powerboats were slowly sinking. "Oh, God, why did we ever— Ethan!" She could just barely make out her brother's face twenty yards or so away. "Are you guys okay?"

191

"Laura's knocked out," Ethan called back, his voice strained with fear and exertion, "but I've got her. I'm going to swim back to the dock."

Sam swam over to help Ethan. Elli kicked off her waterlogged sneakers, then began breast-stroking through the dark water toward shore. The night suddenly seemed deathly quiet and still. Ahead of her, she could see a golden head and pale arms lifting in sure, strong strokes. Charlotte was already halfway to shore. *Did you get what you wanted, Charlotte?* Elli wondered bitterly. *Are you happy now?*

By the time she reached shore, she was winded and chilled. Her heart pounding, she focused on the shapes of Ethan, Sam, and Laura. It seemed like an eternity before the boys waded into the shallows, Laura's limp body supported between them. "She's still unconscious," Elli declared, her voice quavering.

Sam had his face close to Laura's, his fingers on the pulse in her neck. "She's not breathing!" he shouted. "Quick, lay her down. We've got to do CPR! I'll phone for help."

As Sam ran into the darkness, Ethan nearly flung Laura onto the sand, then straddled her prone body, placing his mouth over hers. Elli watched, full of dread, as he forced air into Laura's lungs, then drew back in order to press down on her chest. Laura's eyes were open, her face white. Arms flung out to the side, she looked like one of the dolls in Elli's cedar chest. Meanwhile Charlotte stood at a distance, watching. "Breathe, Laura," Elli whispered. "Breathe."

Moments later, Sam returned, and Ethan looked up in despair. "Nothing," Ethan cried hoarsely. "It's not working!"

"Keep trying," Sam urged. "The emergency workers will be here any second."

Again Ethan placed his mouth over Laura's in a gruesome parody of a kiss. *A last kiss—a good-bye kiss.* Elli pushed the thought from her mind. One breath, two, three, and still Laura didn't respond. "Help him, Sam," Elli cried in desperation.

"He's as good at this as anybody," said Sam, his voice tense. "There's nothing I can do."

Ethan worked feverishly over Laura's body. Sirens sounded in the distance. The noise grew louder, and within seconds the emergency team had reached Laura. Ethan sat up, his arms dropping limply to his sides. A moan of despair ripped from his throat. "It's no use. She's . . . she's dead."

Elli's knees buckled as the emergency team surrounded Laura. She sagged against Sam, turning from the horrible sight. *Please do something,* she pleaded silently, clinging to the last thread of hope. But the emergency workers couldn't revive Laura.

Elli realized that lights had come on in some of the cottages. People were racing down to the dock, drawn by the noise of the boats, the crash, the screams, the sirens. Mrs. Wells and Mr. Ransom arrived just as Ethan staggered to his feet and ran away. The emergency workers were strapping Laura on a stretcher.

"Oh, God," Elli choked out, tears streaming down her face. "I'll never forgive myself. Why did we ever . . ."

Sam wrapped his arms around her. "Shh," he murmured, stroking her wet hair. "It's too late for that. There's nothing we can do."

Elli didn't want his consolation—not now. Not when she could feel her brother's anguish pulsing through the night. "Ethan," she said, pushing Sam away. "Ethan needs me. I have to go to him."

She ran from Sam, searching wildly for her brother. He hadn't returned to Laura. *Where is he?* Elli wondered, spinning in a circle, raking the entire dark scene with her eyes. Then she glimpsed them sitting on the dock, the dark head, the fair head. Charlotte and Ethan.

Her face a blank, white mask, Charlotte cradled Ethan in her arms, rocking him as he sobbed brokenheartedly. "No," Elli whispered. "Not her, Ethan. Don't turn to her."

But he already had. He'd gone to Charlotte, the source of his pain, for comfort. *Just like when she hit him with a hammer when they were children,* Elli thought, her mouth dry with horror and disbelief. *The more pain she causes him, the more he needs her.*

At that moment Charlotte glanced up through a wild tangle of damp golden hair and saw Elli staring. Something flickered in Charlotte's deep blue eyes as their gazes locked. She looked traumatized, but also . . . triumphant? Elli turned away, bruised and heartsick. Slowly she walked back toward Laura's lifeless body, the tears once again streaming like rain down her face.

13

"But I don't see why you took the blame for it," Elli told Ethan incredulously the next day.

They'd all spent a harrowing, sleepless night. An ambulance had taken Laura's body away from Silver Beach. Then the police had arrived and fired questions at the survivors of the boat crash. An inquest was scheduled, at which it was more than likely that Laura's death would be determined accidental. There was only one unknown: Would charges of negligent homicide be brought?

When Ethan didn't answer her, Elli gripped his arm and shook him. His coffee sloshed onto the floor. "You lied, Ethan," she persisted. "You said your boat caused the crash. You said powerboat chicken was your idea. Why?"

Ethan looked at Elli with dull eyes. "Does it matter?" he asked, his voice flat, expressionless. "She's dead."

"You're protecting Charlotte," Elli declared sharply.

"Does it matter?" Ethan repeated, turning away.

When Laura's parents arrived a few hours later, Elli and Mrs. Wells met them at the door. For a long moment the two mothers embraced, both crying. Elli stood to the side, shifting her weight from one foot to the other, wishing she were on another continent, another planet—anywhere but right here, right now.

Mr. McIver was a tall, handsome man, but his face was ashen and he stood with his shoulders slumped. "Where's Ethan?" he asked Elli. "We thought he might want to come home with us. For the . . ." His voice broke on the word. "Funeral."

"I—I don't know where he is," Elli confessed. "I'll look for him."

But even as she ran from the house she knew she wouldn't find him, because he didn't want to be found. She pounded on the door of Briarwood, but received no answer, and the door was locked. "Coward," Elli muttered, anger bubbling through the sorrow. He'd run away—he was hiding from the McIvers. And worst of all, he was with Charlotte. Elli was sure of it.

Ethan showed up just as the McIvers were preparing to leave Silver Beach. Sitting with Sam on the porch, Elli watched her brother speaking to Laura's parents. He shook his head at their invitation to return to Winnetka with them, then embraced them quickly and hurried off again.

"I still can't believe it," said Sam, one arm firmly around Elli's trembling shoulders as Laura's parents drove away.

"It's a nightmare," she agreed, "only it's a nightmare that's going to go on and on. We're never going to wake up and be free of it."

"I should've known better," said Sam, his voice shaking. "I should've put a stop to it. It's my fault."

"*Your* fault?" Elli blinked at him, her eyes wide and still wet with tears. "You weren't the one driving the boat. It was Charlotte—all Charlotte, from the beginning."

"It was my boat, so I'm responsible," Sam insisted.

"No," Elli cried. "Just because Ethan's stupid enough to try to take the blame doesn't mean you have to let her off the hook, too. Doesn't anyone see this for what it really is?" When Sam looked at her blankly, she continued in a tortured whisper, "It was *murder,* Sam. Revenge plain and simple—a death for a death. Charlotte blames my family for her mother's suicide, so she killed Laura, whom she hated anyway for stealing Ethan from her. Don't you *see*?"

Sam shook his head. "That's crazy, Elli. It

198

was an accident. Charlotte didn't plan it. We're all equally at fault."

Deep in her heart, Elli knew Sam was right about one thing: They'd all played the game willingly, so they shared responsibility for the consequences. But she couldn't believe he was so blind to Charlotte's motives. "If she didn't want something bad to happen, why did she suggest powerboat chicken in the first place?" Elli challenged. "You don't think it's a little suspicious?"

"Well . . . no. Not really."

Elli stared at Sam, her heart thumping painfully. "Whose side are you on? Why are you protecting her?"

"It's not a question of sides," Sam said defensively. "It was an accident, a tragic accident. And I'm not protecting anyone."

Hearing the cold edge in his voice, Elli suddenly recalled her conversation with Sam the previous day. She'd been sure he was hiding something from her—holding something back, being less than honest. *And Charlotte's always had a thing for Sam,* Elli thought, dizzy with fatigue and confusion. *Is he hiding something about Charlotte, something that's gone on between them?*

"You're as pathetic as Ethan. She's got you under her spell," Elli accused him. "Is there something going on that I should know about?"

"Snap out of it, Elli." Sam grasped her arm and

gave her a gentle shake. "Don't be ridiculous."

Elli wrenched her arm away. "There is some-thing," she cried, too upset to care if she was being irrational. The reality of Laura's death crashed down on her, and she felt herself falling, falling, into some black, bottomless void, with no one to hold on to, no one to trust. "What other secrets have you been keeping from me, Sam?"

"Elli—"

But Elli spun on her heel and ran back into the house, slamming the door behind her.

The late afternoon sun falling on the deserted west beach of Blueberry Island was hazy and warm. Ethan lay in the sand with his head on Charlotte's lap. She stroked his hair, rubbed his temples. "Close your eyes," she advised. "You must be so beat. You'll feel better if you sleep."

Ethan looked up at her as she bent over him. He *was* tired, bone tired. But he couldn't close his eyes. He was afraid to fall asleep, afraid to tear his gaze from Charlotte's face. She was the only thing standing between him and utter dark-ness. "Hold me, Char," Ethan whispered, sitting up and reaching for her. "Please hold me."

Charlotte wrapped her arms around him, murmuring softly, "It's okay. I'm here."

He pressed his face against her shoulder, squeezing his eyes shut. And the images came, as he knew they would. Sam's motorboat slicing across the dark water toward him, the moment of impact—and, on the shore, Laura's white, white face. The stillness of her body, the chill of her dead skin.

"I did it," Ethan moaned, grief and guilt exploding to the surface. "I loved her and now she's . . . Why did I make her ride in the boat with me? Why did I bring her to Silver Beach at all? Oh, God, if only I could go back in time and—"

"Hush," Charlotte commanded. She placed her hands on either side of his face. "Don't torture yourself like that. You can't go back, so there's no point even thinking about it. Think about *now,* Ethan." Her voice dropped to a seductive whisper. "Think about *me.*"

Her warm, soft lips were on his and they were kissing. Ethan's arms tightened around her body; he held on like a drowning man clinging to a life ring. And as the kiss grew longer and deeper, as they fell back on the blanket, the past did fade away. Or rather, the past year. This was like a return to a different past—to the previous summer, the summer of Charlotte. The summer before Laura.

The images intruded again—Laura's sweet, innocent face, her parents' stark grief. Ethan pushed them away. Losing himself in Charlotte was his only hope of escape and forgetfulness. His fingers fumbled with the buttons of Charlotte's shirt. "I need you so much," he said hoarsely. "Promise you won't leave me."

Charlotte pressed her body close to his. "I'll take care of you. No one will come between us ever again."

A week since Laura's death, Elli thought, staring listlessly out the living room window at the pouring rain. Every day dragged on for an eternity, and her loneliness and depression were a thousand times worse because she and Sam weren't speaking to each other. All she wanted was to go home. Would summer never end?

No charges were being pressed against Ethan or any of the others involved in the boat accident; the inquest had been a routine procedure. *Now we just get on with our lives,* Elli thought. *But how?* Just then she saw a figure crossing the lawn toward the house. He didn't have an umbrella; his hair hung in dripping strands and his wet clothes clung to his lean body. Elli met Ethan at the door. "Where have you been?"

"Charlotte and I got caught in the rain," he mumbled, pushing past her toward the stairs. "Need to change into some dry clothes."

"Ethan," Elli called after him.

Reluctantly he turned to face her. "What?"

"Ethan, we haven't even really talked since . . ." Suddenly she felt as cold as he looked. How could she tell her brother how afraid she was for him? "Since . . ."

He put his foot on the bottom stair. "What's to talk about?"

"Ethan, this has got to stop."

"What has got to stop?"

"Don't play dumb," she snapped. "Ethan, how can you? How can you get back together with her when she's the one who—"

"Charlotte didn't do anything," Ethan interrupted, his eyes flashing. "Stop trying to make her the villain."

Elli wanted to slap her brother hard—anything to bring him back to reality, to shake him free of Charlotte's influence. Instead she pummeled him with words, the harshest and bluntest she could muster. "She killed Laura, Ethan. You can run away from the McIvers, and you can run away from me, but you can't run away from that. She *killed* Laura!"

Ethan's jaw tightened. For a moment Elli thought she'd broken through—if nothing else, they'd roll up their sleeves and have a good, down-and-dirty fight. But then, without saying another word, Ethan turned his back on her and climbed the stairs three at a time.

When his bedroom door slammed, Elli let out a defeated sigh. Her grandmother had stepped into the hall. "It's no use, Nana," Elli said. "Charlotte's got him again, and she'll never let him go."

Mrs. Chapman slipped an arm around her

granddaughter's waist. "Ethan has to grieve in his own way. He'll come to his senses."

"But it's . . . it's . . ." *Wrong. Evil.* She couldn't say the words—they were too extreme—but it was what she was feeling. "After what Charlotte did, if he ever really loved Laura . . . how *could* he?"

"He's young, and he's wounded. Deeply wounded," said Mrs. Chapman. "He's not thinking, and to tell you the truth, I believe very firmly that there are times when it's foolish to think too much. Maybe for Ethan this is one of them."

"But you can't *approve* of him getting back together with Charlotte, under the circumstances!" Elli exclaimed.

Mrs. Chapman lifted her thin shoulders. "It's not for me to judge, dear."

After her grandmother disappeared into the master suite, Elli pushed open the front door and crossed the porch. Running down onto the lawn, she tilted her face to the rain. She wanted to be soaked to the skin, cleansed, healed.

And the rain helped. It cooled her skin, cleared her mind. But her heart remained weary and sore and confused. She thought of the big house behind her—of Ethan inside it, locked in his own room, of her mother and grandmother. *We live under the same roof, but we're all so alone, so separate,* Elli thought. What had happened to her family? By the end of summer, would there be anything left of it?

*　　*　　*

The late August morning dawned cool and fresh after the rain. The air that fluttered the curtains of Charlotte's bedroom carried a promise of fall. She woke up smiling and hummed to herself as she slipped her arms into the sleeves of an old silk bathrobe. *Summer's over,* Charlotte thought, *and it didn't turn out so badly, considering how it started.*

Downstairs, she sauntered into the kitchen. "Morning, Dad," she said boldly, reaching for the coffeepot and pouring herself a cup.

Mr. Ransom started at the sight of his daughter. "I thought I told you once before never to wear that robe," he snapped.

"You did," Charlotte conceded, sipping her coffee, "but you know what? I'm going to wear it anyway."

Mr. Ransom raised his eyebrows in astonishment. "What did you say?"

Charlotte knew that tone—overbearing, ominous. In the past, she'd always cowered before her father when he'd spoken to her like that; she'd been afraid of his temper, abject in her desire to please him. Not anymore. "I'm going to wear Mom's robe anyway," Charlotte repeated coolly. "You can't tell me what to do, Dad. You have absolutely no rights over me."

His face darkened. "I'm your father. You're underage and you live in my house."

She shrugged, unimpressed. "None of that means a thing. Know why? Because when you cheated on Mom nine years ago with Mrs. Wells, you stopped being a husband to her, and when she drowned herself because of what you did, you stopped being a father to me."

"I won't take this from you, Charlotte," Mr. Ransom warned.

She laughed. "Then you don't have to listen. But I'm not going to stop talking." Her expression grew serious. "I'm not going to lie down and die, Dad. I'm not Mom. I've figured out something she didn't—how to take what I want from life, instead of always losing out. I love being alive, even though I'm stuck in this tomb of a house with you for a father."

"Good morning, Eleanor," Charlotte sang outside the boathouse a few hours later, still feeling the triumph from her conversation with her father that morning. "Going for one last row?"

Elli nodded without speaking.

Charlotte tilted her head to one side. "But you're all by yourself. Where's the boyfriend?"

"He's not my boyfriend," Elli muttered, yanking at the door of the shed where the canoes and paddles were stored.

"I see. You're on the outs." Charlotte couldn't suppress her delight. "Too bad."

"If you don't mind . . ." Elli turned her back pointedly.

Charlotte followed her into the boathouse. "Well, you know, if you want some company, Ethan and I would be happy to join you."

Elli whirled around, her eyes flashing. "I would rather die," she declared hotly.

Charlotte smiled. "Now, isn't that a funny choice of words."

Elli lifted a hand to her throat as if she were choking. "I can't believe you, Charlotte Ransom. How can you act so . . . blatant? So proud of what you did to Laura?"

"What *I* did?" Charlotte raised her eyebrows innocently. "You were there, Elli. It was an accident. You're not saying I caused it on purpose?"

Elli didn't answer, but her skepticism was written all over her face.

Well, whatever, Charlotte thought. *Let her think what she wants to think.* "Have a nice time, Elli," she said, breezing back out of the boathouse.

She stopped in the clubhouse to buy a soda from the vending machine, and then continued on toward the tennis courts, where Ethan would be waiting for her. The morning sparkled around her: dewy emerald-green grass, a lake like a mirror, a brilliant blue sky. Charlotte thought Silver Beach had never looked so beautiful. There was no question that, in the final moments, the game of summer had turned around in her favor and now she was winning, hands down. *No, Elli,* Charlotte mused, *I didn't intend for Laura to die, no matter what you think. But this revenge couldn't taste sweeter if I had planned it.*

Ordinarily it was the saddest day of the year—the official final day of summer vacation, the day they loaded the car, closed up the cottage, and drove home to Winnetka. This year the sadness was of a different variety, immeasurably deeper and more profound. It weighed them all down, slowing their steps as they moved around the house packing suitcases and fastening shutters. *The car ride is going to be unbearable,* Elli thought as she shut and locked her bedroom windows, then pulled the curtains. Two months earlier, four cheerful people had driven north to Silver Beach in the Range Rover. Only three of them were returning home.

When her room was neat, Elli lugged her suitcases downstairs and dumped them in the hall on her way to the kitchen. Her grandmother was at the stove, scrambling eggs in one skillet while bacon sizzled in another.

"Nana, what are you doing?" asked Elli. "This is supposed to be a cold-cereal, make-as-little-mess-as-possible morning."

"I know it is," Mrs. Chapman said, "but I just had a hunch we'd all do better today if we started out with a hot breakfast. I've mustered the rest of the troops—go on in and I'll bring the eggs in a minute."

Sure enough, Ethan and Mrs. Wells were already in the breakfast room, pouring coffee and buttering toast. "Good morning," Elli said, taking a seat.

Her mother passed her a cup of coffee. "Morning, Elli."

Ethan was slumped in his chair, staring morosely at his empty plate. *What's the matter with you? You're not psyched to get away from this place, after everything that happened?* Elli wanted to say, but she bit her tongue. It was all too obvious that Ethan was beginning to suffer his annual pangs of withdrawal from Charlotte. *And probably the pangs are sharper than ever—he's more dependent on her now, after Laura's death, than he's ever been.*

Mrs. Chapman entered, bearing a china platter piled with eggs and bacon. "Umm, that smells fabulous, Mother," said Mrs. Wells. "You shouldn't have gone to so much trouble, but I'm glad you did."

The platter made its way around the table.

210

"You know, it's funny," Elli remarked as they ate. "I don't remember the last time we all sat down for a meal together. Better late than never, I guess."

Her mother looked guilty; Mrs. Chapman looked sorrowful; Ethan's eyes remained downcast.

"Thanks for humoring me," said Mrs. Chapman. "I know you're all eager to get on the road, but I wanted to keep you with me for a few minutes longer. You're my family, and I'll miss you."

Even though he'd barely touched his eggs, Ethan tossed his napkin on the table, preparing to stand up. "Speaking of leaving, Mom, what's our schedule?"

"Well, actually, that's up to you and Elli," said Mrs. Wells. "I might not— I don't think I'll—" She didn't finish the sentence.

Ethan frowned. "What?"

Mrs. Wells bit her lip. "I guess I should have mentioned this sooner. You see, I've been thinking about . . . no, I've decided." Her tone became more resolute. "I'm not going back to Winnetka with you today."

"What?" Elli dropped her fork with a clatter. "What are you talking about, Mom?"

"I'm not going back to Winnetka," Mrs. Wells repeated. "I've decided to stay on through the fall."

"Here?" Ethan was baffled. "In the cottage by yourself?"

Mrs. Wells shook her head, and suddenly Elli felt sick. She knew what her mother was going

211

to say next. "No, not here. I'll be next door. At Briarwood, with Holling."

Elli stared at her plate, unable to touch her food or to look up at her family. For long moments, they sat in stunned silence.

Finally Ethan burst out, "I can't believe this. What about me and Elli? What about . . . home?"

"It's okay. You won't be alone. I spoke with your father a few days ago," said Mrs. Wells. "He'll move back into the Winnetka house for the duration. That will be fun for you, won't it?"

"The duration. What does *that* mean?" Elli asked sharply. "When are you coming back, Mom? Are you ever coming back?"

"Of course I'm coming back," Mrs. Wells replied, looking from Elli to Ethan. "Two months." Her tone was bright, false. "These cottages aren't very well winterized—when it starts to get cold, I'll be home in a hurry."

Ethan shook his head. "Jeez, this is great," he said bitterly. "What they call a custody arrangement, huh? Stick us with Dad whether he wants us or not, until you feel like being a parent again."

Shoving back his chair, he bolted from the room. Mrs. Wells hurried after him, her face distraught. "Ethan, wait. Let's talk about this. Honey, please . . ."

Elli and Mrs. Chapman were left staring at each other. Elli couldn't help laughing at her grandmother's expression. "Don't tell me *you're* shocked, Nana. Nothing ever surprises you!"

Mrs. Chapman smiled ruefully. "I didn't see this coming," she admitted.

Elli sighed, not quite sure what she was feeling. *Ethan's close to tears—I should be devastated, too.* But somehow she wasn't. In fact, she felt strangely relieved. It would be easier not living with her mother for a while. They'd all have time to cool down, adjust to new realities.

Elli looked at her grandmother. "It's weird, isn't it, Nana? Something happened between Mom and Mr. Ransom nine years ago, and now it's started again. And it's the same with Ethan and Charlotte. For better or for worse, they keep coming back to each other. Like it's all . . . inevitable."

"If there's one true lesson to be learned from human experience, it's that history repeats itself, though usually with a twist," her grandmother agreed. "We imagine we can neatly divide things up into past, present, and future, but it doesn't work that way. The past won't stay buried."

Elli sipped her lukewarm coffee. *History repeats itself; the past won't stay buried.* What did that mean for the future? How many more secrets would surface in Silver Beach?

Ethan locked his bedroom door, not answering his mother's pleas. After a minute, he heard her footsteps retreating down the hall.

213

Crossing the room, he sat down at his desk and opened the top drawer. Amid the jumble of pens and paper clips, old magazines and notebook paper, he found the small jewelry box he'd opened earlier that summer. He tucked the box into his pocket, then started to slide the drawer shut. Something else caught his eye, and he reached again into the drawer. A photograph.

He'd taken the picture of Laura at the beginning of the summer. She was standing on the beach, the wind blowing her light brown hair. So sweet, so lovely, so *alive.*

Ethan's eyes welled up. Quickly he shoved the photo to the back of the drawer and slammed it shut. He wouldn't think of her. He *couldn't* think of her, of her death. He had to focus on the present—on Charlotte. A minute later, he was knocking on the door of Briarwood.

The front hall of the cottage was littered with trunks and suitcases; Charlotte was returning that day to Bedford Hall, her downstate boarding school. "Can you believe all this junk?" she asked Ethan. "Come on, let's get out of here. Otherwise my dad'll expect us to help him load the car."

They ran out of the house and across the lawn toward the lake. The beach was deserted in either direction; most of the summer families had already packed up and departed. They crouched behind a grassy dune, and Ethan threw his arms around her. "I love you, Char," he said, burying his face in her sweet-smelling blond hair. "I'll miss you like crazy. Promise . . ."

"Promise what?"

"It won't be like last year." His voice cracked with emotion. "When you didn't write or call." *And I fell in love with Laura. And if I hadn't fallen in love with Laura, I wouldn't have brought her to Silver Beach. She'd be alive today.*

"You're mine and I'm yours," Charlotte said simply. "We'll stay in touch, I promise. You can visit me at Bedford Hall."

"And next summer we'll be together again," Ethan said. "Say it."

"We'll be together," Charlotte repeated, "every day and every night."

They started to kiss, and Ethan pulled Charlotte down on the sand. "I have something for you," he murmured.

"Here?" she teased. "In broad daylight?"

He laughed, producing the small box. "No. This." Charlotte opened the box and removed the slim band of silver set with an opal. "It's not much," he said, "but it means—it means forever, Charlotte, because what I feel for you is . . ." How could he put it into words? How could he explain that his irrational, unstoppable love for Charlotte was greater than ever, because it had swallowed up his love for Laura—that different, gentler love?

He slipped the ring on her finger.

"I'll never take it off," Charlotte promised.

Ethan gazed into her eyes, sinking into their clear blue depths, memorizing every feature of her face, her complexion, the glint of her hair. He ran his hands over her shoulders, down her arms, her waist, her back, so that he could take the memory of her away with him in his fingertips. So that her image would always be uppermost in his mind.

Ethan knew he would never again look at another girl. Charlotte Ransom owned him, body and soul.

The Range Rover was packed. Elli had said an awkward good-bye to her mother and a more freely emotional good-bye to Mrs. Chapman. Her grandmother had left an hour earlier for her winter home in South Carolina.

Charlotte and her father had departed for Bedford Hall, so Ethan had no reason to linger. "Ready when you are," he said to Elli.

She jingled the car keys. "Yeah. Okay."

Just as she was about to slide behind the wheel, Elli stepped away from the Range Rover and slammed the driver's-side door. *I didn't say good-bye to him. Even if we're mad at each other, even if we've broken up, I should say good-bye.* "There's just one more thing I have to do," she told her brother. "Be right back."

She hurried on foot down the gravel road, her thoughts in a tumult. What if Sam wasn't home? What if *he'd* already left without saying good-bye? Elli realized her heart was pounding with hope. She wanted more than just a chance to say good-bye; she wanted to straighten things out. No matter what had happened, Sam's friendship was worth too much to Elli to let it slip away without a fight.

As she neared Eagle Point she broke into a run. By the time she rang the bell, she was breathless. When Sam himself answered the door, she nearly burst into tears of relief. "Oh, it's you. I'm so glad," she panted. "I was afraid you'd—that I—that we—"

Somehow they were in each other's arms and to Elli's astonishment, Sam was showering her with kisses. "Oh, Elli, we've been acting like such idiots," he declared.

She kissed him back. "It was all my fault. I'm sorry. I shouldn't have lashed out because of what you said about . . . the accident. About Charlotte."

"It's been awful staying away from you. I don't know what I was trying to prove," said Sam.

Elli shook her head. "I was totally unreasonable. I was awful to you."

"You were upset. You just needed my support."

Elli squeezed his hand in her own. "We should've given each other the benefit of the doubt," she concluded.

Sam held her tightly. "But we're both so damned stubborn," he said with a wry laugh. "Not to mention pretty good at getting our signals crossed."

"Yeah, but we're also good at making up," Elli whispered, lifting her lips to his once more.

For a few minutes they lost themselves in passionate kisses. Then, reluctantly, Elli pulled away. "Ethan's waiting for me," she explained. "I really should go."

Sam brushed the hair back from her face and gazed into her eyes. "Not before you make a promise," he insisted, his tone serious.

"What kind of promise?" she asked, her hands clasped around his waist.

"You have to promise that even though it's the end of summer, this is just the beginning for us. That next summer . . ."

Elli smiled, her eyes brighter than they'd been in a long time. They had been through more than their share of sorrow and tragedy, but there was always a new year, a chance for a fresh start. "Next summer," she vowed.